The stars. A hundred billion pinpricks of blue-white light puncturing the infinitely black canvas of the void that separates them from each other. They are not al

In between, around and even touching them, are the nebu every shape. Towers of burning orange and red, giant spla expanses of hazy fading green and yellow. They are not al

Moving through them are the graceful comets, trailing dust tails thousands of reflecting stray starlight in glorious ghostly auras. They are joined by the cold, heavily-cratered, aimless rogue planets. Absorbing all light, letting none out, they pass through the void: stealthy, homeless loners. They are not alone.

As the light from the burning stars and radiant nebulae plays out across the universe and its spinning galaxies, it falls onto the objects caught in solar gravities. Dead, barren asteroids turn and spin of their own accord, forming belts and necklaces and clouds. Sometimes they break free of their invisible moorings and find new homes over immense, rainbow-streaked gas giants. In the thick, chaotic atmospheres rage storms of unimaginable size and colour mixtures, lit by lightning on their hosts' dark sides. They are not alone.

Joining them in their great orbital journeys around the stars are smaller orbs, every one unique. Some are as dead as their asteroid brethren, with no atmospheres to breathe. Others are cloaked in thick choking clouds of every colour and element. Some strike a balance. On their surfaces entities move, lumbering, sliding, gliding, flying and walking. See from orbit, fields of lights of every spectrum shine back out at the other inhabitants of the void. And scattered throughout the universe, almost indiscernible to the casual observer, objects move between all of them with more than random movement.

"They are coming!"

*   *   *

Alanar jerked violently from his peaceful sleep with a gasp. He was covered in a disgustingly clammy cold sweat that would make any attempt at drifting back impossible. He looked out the window to his left and groaned quietly. The sun had risen enough that its light was slicing through the gaps between his building's fellow high-rises. Now even a futile attempt at slumber was not only impossible, but pointless. He was only moments away from a synth-sym wake-up call.

He hoisted himself to sit on the edge of his bed, facing away from the sun, letting it warm the hairless grey-blue skin on his back. Both of his left arms scratched absently near the spine area where small blunt spikes stuck out vertically every few centimetres. Collecting his thoughts and yawning, he stood up, completely naked, revealing a pair of small vestigial legs below the back of his knees as he walked out of the bedroom towards a smaller cubical.

Standing inside, Alanar touched a panel and seconds later several dozen steady jets of peridot fluid drenched his skin from above, all angled towards him. A split second later an ultrasonic screech assaulted his senses.

"Shut up!" he yelled, continuing to let the liquid rain over him while he tried to refocus.

The screech stopped, replaced by a gentle but attentive male voice emanating from nowhere in particular.

"...Chancellor stressing the importance of respecting inter-civilisation law and the Confederation's own simultaneously. In other news –"

"Isolate and distil relevant segments," Alanar grunted, rubbing his arms vigorously.

"Programme initiated," an indifferent ambient male voice answered.

Alanar turned around, washing his back now and loosening stiff muscles. His eyes had quickly now adjusted to block the glare of the dawn sun. He could see anti-gravity pods moving among the buildings and high above, leaving blurry distortion trails in their wakes for a few moments which quickly faded to nothingness.

Beyond that he could just see a huge starship rising into the sky, water sloughing off it in torrents as it did so, a rainbow shimmering below it, the sunlight glancing off its armour in every direction. He smiled a little and recovered some semblance of a good mood.

Alanar had lived here for two months and was yet to tire of that sight. No matter how often he saw it, the vision never failed to impress and amuse him. Then again, undersea military bases only existed on two planets in the whole of the Confederation.

"Programme complete," the second male voice reported.

"Present results. Shower off."

The jets stopped and a towel rack emerged from a side panel. He grabbed it on his way out and began drying himself as the voice read out several lines of news reports.

"HYCAP AM's headlines are as follows: the situation on the Winn Winn-Tardig border, the Oceana Conference and the interventionist protests in the capital today. Not much change from yesterday other than the reports of a battle on the border near Second Hygra."

Alanar wrapped the towel around his waist.

He swore. "What was our response?"

"The Confederation's or Hygra's?"

"The Confederation's."

"The Presidium condemned both sides and promised assistance to the survivors. HYCAP AM also suspects a military force may be dispatched to the colony."

He opened a chest of drawers and pulled out undergarments, carefully sliding them up his calves, over the minor legs and to his waist, followed by a pair of foot coverings. A wardrobe was opened, exposing three military uniforms.

"HYCAP AM *suspects*?"

Navy-blue trousers were hauled on.

"An unofficial source inside the Hygran Defence Directorate. There is apparently talk of a joint Hygran-Confederation force being assembled."

A quad-sleeved navy-blue shirt was pulled on and smoothed out.

"Really?" laughed the alien, fastening his black belt. "I imagine the non-interventionists will have a field day with that."

Alanar sat on the bed to lace up his boots – pitch black, heavy-looking things that added nearly half an inch to his already substantial height. As he finished, a sound like wind chimes in the breeze was played.

"You have a call incoming from Confederation Navy Base Hygra, Vice-Admiral Suchovskaya's office," the voice said.

He walked over to the wardrobe and removed an overcoat the same colour as his shirt.

"Let her through."

A slightly pixelated hologram of a stern-looking woman with long black hair materialised in the middle of the room. She was dressed in a uniform much like Alanar's, only with a cap with blue braids running around her cap brim, coat cuffs and across the coat shoulders and left breast pocket.

"Officer Alanar," she said, saluting, prompting a similar gesture from him. "Thank you for being so prompt."

"Not a problem, Vice-Admiral," he replied, fetching his own cap. "I was just on my way to the Directorate."

The woman nodded, her expression not shifting.

"You may wish to change that, Officer. Myself, Director Shaxar and the Prime Minister are at the Navy base. Your presence is required."

He saluted again.

"Yes, Vice-Admiral."

"Good man. Have an away kit packed. You'll be out of town for a while."

The hologram flared away. Alanar pulled on his cap.

"You heard the lady. Standard away kit settings."

"Affirmative," the voice said.

He made his way out of the apartment and into a transit shaft he shared with others on this floor, stepping into the empty shaft and falling twenty storeys to the ground level. As soon as he began descending a gravity manipulation device secured him, allowing a certain amount of freefall at safe speed and without the danger of a messy death.

As soon as he'd made it to his target level, the officer made a beeline for the rotating doors. The street outside was already full of pedestrians going about their business. All vehicles were suspended overhead, allowing complete free-flow of people. Normally, Alanar would have bobbed along in the hubbub towards the Defence Directorate, but today was different. He had three of the most powerful people in the sector waiting for him.

Inside his head, attached to his brain, a bio-mechanical mass was stretched out, extending its tendrils into his mind. A synthetic symbiote. A genetically-engineered, cybernetically-enhanced organism that bonded the minds of their users to the info-net and enabled various devices and vehicles to be used at any time with ease. With a directed thought he sent a message to the nearest taxi a-grav pod, asking for pick-up and transport to the Confederation base.

Exactly fifteen seconds later, a yellow and black chequered pod came to rest a metre above him and extended a ramp down. As he climbed aboard he sent a command to the pod's computer core that let him override its civilian functions. It would make the transit much easier.

The moment the ramp closed, the pod shot up ten metres into the air and sped in the direction of the seafront. Inside, Alanar accessed the sensor nodes to show the approach inside his mind. He saw the bustling dock area where the hundreds of leisure and commercial vessels of the Hygran capital city were going about their business. Despite the planet's high technology, it continued to invest heavily in its traditional industries, an act which caused surprisingly little disruption given the close proximity to the starship take-off and landing areas in the waters beneath them.

In less than two minutes the pod was over the open sea, hovering directly above the complex below according to Alanar's memory. A query was broadcast from the central command station's communications area, requesting an identify friend-foe code which he returned. The officer also uploaded a programme into the taxi pod's core alongside his control link. It was essentially a virus on a countdown timer that would wipe all record of the journey beyond the time and a few other credentials. Despite the benign nature of the base and it being peace time, the security of Confederation military assets remained essential.

The IFF recognition message was sent back in three seconds flat and instantly Alanar sent the pod into a nose dive into the water. At first only a few fish and rays of sunlight were visible, then some seaweed, fish shoals and the odd predator. Then nothing as the light faded out further down. He didn't adjust the sensors. It would only take a moment.

Suddenly, a galaxy of lights appeared before him, growing brighter as it approached at speed. The scene presented was awe-inspiring: a vast layout of various modules, connection corridors and domes that made up the shipyards, offices, quarters and various other parts of the dozens of square kilometres that was Navy base Hygra. From his approach vector he could see the profiles of three Confederation Navy swordships berthed below him, doubtless more would be nearby.

Each craft was three kilometres long and shaped like an ancient weapon, common in many cultures in the Confederation, armed with terrifying firepower that could inflict immense destruction upon any opposition. Without doubt, they were one of the main reasons for the long years of virtually uninterrupted peace in the Confederation.

The taxi continued onwards towards a huge dome at the heart of this artificial reef of activity. The central command hub. A section of the lower dome slid away to reveal a shielded bay where tens of fighters and gunships sat behind a panel of blue-force field. The pod hit the field, which formed almost a complete bubble around it before bursting just as it closed, letting in but a few droplets of salty water.

As the pod settled on the decking, Alanar disconnected from it and exited via a side panel to be greeted by two Marines in full heavy-looking, body-concealing armour suits and shell helmets. One was clearly Hygran from its four arms holding two kinetic slam rifles. The other, judging by its two and a half metre height and tank-like build, had to be a Kin-Sai. The Marines were flanking a Human dressed in uniform with gold braids as opposed to Alanar's silver. The officer saluted and Alanar recognised him almost immediately from countless online exchanges.

"At ease, Officer Alanar," the man said, extending a hand. "Captain Thomas Lamont, Vice-Admiral Suchovskaya's deputy. It is good to meet you in the flesh after all this time coordinating over the info-net."

Alanar shook the offered hand.

"Thank you, Captain. Is there a problem?"

Thomas glanced briefly at the Marines.

"No, Officer. It's just a bit busy at the moment and the extra muscle might get us to the mission planning room faster."

Alanar's eyes widened a little in confusion. The planning room was only used for coming up with ways to achieve tactical objectives.

"I see," he said, nodding. "Shall we join the brass?"

The Captain smiled warmly.

"We shall indeed. Walk with me."

All four walked quickly towards the exit into the hallway of the hub, one Marine behind, the other in front, clearing the way and giving them space. Captain Lamont had been right. Everywhere there were people rushing about with various pieces of equipment and orders. It seemed the whole base was getting ready for something big.

"Don't worry, Officer. You'll have all your questions answered in due course."

"I've never seen so much activity at the base before," Alanar replied, looking around. "Star Haven and Centralis seem quiet next to this."

"Well, they're not submerged, but we are busy, yes. No accidents yet, though, which is good."

They squeezed past two Kin-Sai carrying a large case of KSRs. Alanar narrowly avoided a face of wiry fur.

"You'd have thought they'd make the corridors bigger for this," he commented.

The Captain thought for a moment.

"Well, you have to bear in mind the history of the place. Centaurians are a lot thinner than most races and hadn't enslaved the Kin-Sai during the Founder's War. Usually, it's not this much of a problem."

A Talan scuttled across the ceiling at speed, making a skittering sound with its six segmented legs.

"Well, some seem to have found a solution."

Thomas snorted.

"Attention all hands! Attention all hands!" a loud, urgent voice announced over the public announcement system. "All morphic warheads must be loaded and prepped in T-minus two hours and counting. Captains Lal-ne-vo, Thor'nek and Shuresh are reminded to meet with the Vice-Admiral immediately. That is all."

"The Vice-Admiral?" asked Alanar.

"You'll remember she just got promoted a month ago," explained the Captain. "No name, only rank. It's a tradition for the first year of service. Do you not have anything similar at the Directorate?"

The Officer thought for a moment. Hygrans were usually a very traditional race, especially on the homeworld. The Defence Directorate was littered with banners and busts. Nothing to do with the rank titles, though. Still, tradition was tradition.

"True. All worlds have it, I suppose."

"Oh, you've no idea. If you ever get a chance to choose your next assignment, go to Kin-Sai space. The battlefleet is the most paraded force I've ever seen."

The troop of four came up to the MPR entrance, guarded by two larger than average Human Marines without helmets, instead displaying faces with cybernetic implants in their left ears and eyes. Specialist Marine Operatives. Best in the Corps.

Captain Lamont saluted them abruptly, a gesture not returned by the SMOs, who instead saw right through them. The entrance opened of its own accord, accessed by the operative's synth-syms.

"I'll leave you here, Officer. Good luck," the Captain said, before turning to rejoin the chaos with his Marines.

Alanar stepped through the entrance and saw a large circular table with a hollow centre. The outside was surrounded by beings in several types of uniform and professional dress. He recognised the PM, Vice-Admiral, Hygra's Military Director and the Confederation Ambassador to the Hygran Consensus, Rykeel. There were others there, too. A Talan, Human and Rigellian in Confederation captains' uniforms and seven Hygrans in command dress.

"Officer Alanar," welcomed the Vice-Admiral. "Please sit down and we'll get started."

Somewhat gingerly, the Hygran took the seat between the Confederation and Hygran command staff. He hated being last at meetings, even impromptu ones. As soon as he sat down, a hologram appeared in the hollow centre of the table depicting a female Hygran in an unbraided uniform. She had a black line running through her right eye from temple to jaw line. A Unified Intelligent Personality Entity. This was serious stuff.

"Alright, let's begin," Suchovskaya said. "Needless to say, all the details of this meeting are classified until the official press release when this is all underway."

"As you know, there was an incident earlier today near Second Hygra between Winn Winn insurgents and forces from the Tardig Republican Guard. There were many casualties on both sides and several craft were disabled. What you don't know is that this incident took place inside the Confederation border, specifically just outside the Second Hygra system."

Everyone exchanged looks. The Republic had been struggling to stabilise the former Winn Winn Empire for decades with much success, but fringe Winn Winn elements on the border with the Confederation continued to fight a guerrilla campaign. Until now the war had been confined to the conquered worlds which made the Confederation's intervention questionable. If warships were duelling over the border it made the situation far more complicated.

"Despite the Confederation's policy of non-intervention, the Hygran Consensus will not allow the actions of others to recklessly endanger our Colonist-Citizens," the Prime Minister added. "Especially those on Second Hygra. Therefore, the government has decided to dispatch a force to the colony to reinforce our security staff there. If any further action occurs, its job will be to head off transgressors."

"Which explains the Hygrans here, but not the Confederation staff," stated a Hygran commander. "Why are we not at the Directorate?"

Though rude, Alanar could see her point. He couldn't even explain his own presence here. He was a liaison officer but this seemed like an internal Hygran matter. Of course, he had been wrong before.

"While we cannot intervene militarily in any external conflict," the UIPE Hygran answered, "the Navy is duty-bound by treaty to assist any Tardig vessel in need of assistance in Confederation space. We also have a constitutional obligation to give aid for all those who request it – i.e. the Winn Winn ships crippled in the battle."

"Which is why we're sending in three swordships with escorts," Suchovskaya said, motioning to a hologram nearby with her thumb as it flared against a wall.

It showed a scale model of the fire planet Second Hygra system. Three arrows appeared – two blue, one green and two crosses. One over the colony, another high above the system with the green arrow circling the entire system.

"While the Hygran elements of the fleet patrol around the perimeter of the system," pointed out the Director of Defence, Shaxar, "the Confederation will provide neutral cover for the colony itself against collateral damage and assist the belligerents. That way there's no conflict of interest while we negotiate with the Republic."

Suchovskaya coughed.

"Sorry – while you negotiate, Vice-Admiral," he corrected himself. Jurisdiction could be a real pain sometimes.

"We cannot stress enough that, despite the small number of ships being sent, there is back-up available if fired upon or if things get out or hand," Suchovskaya reassured them. "I've spoken to Admiral Kisugi and he has placed an entire squadron on stand-by should it be needed. However, let's not allow this degenerate into a shooting war. This is a police and rescue mission. Any stupidity on either side will be accounted for."

The same female Hygran snorted.

"Any stupidity will probably come from the Winn Winn," she pointed out. "They are committed to destroying the Republic. Seven HDD ships probably won't be enough to halt any resumption of hostilities."

The Director began to silence her, but the PM cut him off.

"You are right, Ship-Commander Navat. We should be sending more, but our commitment to the evacuation of Nahypra is absorbing the bulk of our military strength. While we are confident our threats should be enough, if not you'll have to cut and run."

"And who'll be handling our cutting and running?" she asked mockingly.

Alanar could not believe her attitude. How had someone so in-your-face managed to get a command? Then he realised why he was there and his world felt very unsteady.

"That's where Officer Alanar comes in," the Vice-Admiral intervened. "As the Navy liaison to the Directorate, he is perfectly placed to gel both sides' operating procedures and operations until we have this issue resolved."

He could feel his mouth slowly dropping open and quickly shut it and nodded, before opening with more control this time.

"Yes, Vice-Admiral."

"Very good. Your rank for the duration of this operation has been elevated to Commodore. Pick your flagship and run things until the Confederation can secure the border again."

While he was the logical choice, Alanar could not help but feel somewhat out of his depth. Despite its relatively small size, the fire power and capabilities of such a fleet were immense. A single swordship could potentially annihilate an entire planet if used wisely. Three with shieldship escorts were capable of cleaving through entire fleets. He'd hoped that his first command might be something lighter and less important.

"Don't worry, Officer. You won't be alone. Morix29 is a legal expert in things like this." Suchovskaya said, apparently sensing his trepidation. She nodded towards the UIPE hologram which smiled brightly. Alanar felt much better already. UIPEs were a rarity in the Confederation. Having one on his side was a great asset.

"I will be your second-in-command, Commodore. If we run into any problems, my information banks are at your disposal. In the meantime I'll handle the Confederation protection operations over Second Hygra," she added.

Maybe this wouldn't be so difficult after all.

"Deployment will take place all at once," Suchovskaya continued. "In three hours the swordships and shieldships assigned to the mission will depart and rendezvous with the Hygran contingent at Hygar Moon. Our news release will state the fleet is engaging in joint manoeuvres. Once you rendezvous the fleet will jump through the Confederation Navy route to the colony to avoid publicity. It should take approximately twenty-seven hours. If we do this right we can secure Second Hygra, the Confederation and maybe help bring this conflict to an end. If there are no more questions, report to your ships – and good luck!"

They all stood, the captains, UIPE and Commodore saluting before making their way out of the room to their various craft and stations. Alanar directed his synth-sym to send a blanket query message to all his subordinates, symbiotes, nano-fibril implants or email accounts, asking for ship manifests and crew lists along with his own addresses and credentials. With only three hours to go, it was essential to get everyone in the know as to what they were doing.

He received immediate replies from all sixteen command staff, fifteen of whom included requests to position the flag on their ship. Ship-Commander Navat was the odd one out in this regard. It was becoming rapidly obvious that the woman was not a great fan of the Confederation or the Hygran response to the incident. The Commodore prayed she would not cause so much trouble once the fleet was in the field.

It took him only a few minutes to reach the officers' social area, navigating through the corridors which seemed to become less anarchic the closer he got to the higher officers' areas. The room had a magnificent view of the swordship docking and maintenance area, or at least part of it.

Few people outside of the base realised the size of the Navy presence on Hygra. Over fifty swordships and their duets of shieldship escorts could be based here at one time with twenty-five more trios still out in space on rotational patrol. In addition to that there were the arms manufactories, training areas and shipyards that were part of the whole ensemble and always abuzz.

No-one was here to see it, though. All the high-ups were away taking part in the cycling up to the operation. Vice-Admiral Suchovskaya seemed to have put the whole base on a standby drill as appropriate cover.

He sat down next to the nearest window and gazed out at the nearest dock rig. Inside was the *Vigilant Watchman*, one of the swordships assigned to his command. The craft was a magnificent piece of engineering design, built to inspire not intimidate. Despite being in the Navy for six years, he had never actually been aboard one.

At the Prime Academy on Star Haven he had learned capabilities, tactics, layout and weapons system management, all in simulations or on shieldships. Swordships were the pride of the Navy and considered a symbol of the Confederation's might across the Galaxy. It was an honour to command one, let alone three. There was an overwhelming temptation to make it his flagship, but he had a feeling the Hygrans might not respond well to such a move.

So he began reviewing the Hygran contingent statistics: four escort destroyers, two light-cruisers and an old Imperial dreadnought. That kind of ship must have been at least five hundred years old. It belonged in a museum, not a professional military force. The Prime Minister hadn't been joking when he said it was all that could be spared. Unfortunately, it was also the most ideal ship in the fleet for his purposes.

An info-net ping displayed in his mind's eye alongside the fleet data. It was Morix29 providing her details. He instantly felt bad for not requesting them. He had been much more concerned with fleet command. He accepted immediately and called her.

In a nanosecond the hologram appeared in front of him, sitting in the chair opposite and holding a glass of orange juice.

"Hello, Commodore, how can I help?" she asked, smiling that brilliant smile.

"I want to plan the fleet layout with you. After all, we are the highest in the command chain. If anything happens to me, you'll need to take over."

"And you forgot to request my email address and you felt bad."

Alanar wasn't sure if he should agree with or admonish the UIPE. Clearly, she wasn't protocol friendly.

"Sorry, Commodore. I've been in the business for one hundred and seventy years. I learned to dispense with protocol with high-ups a while ago and I'm very good at reading emotions."

"Let's just keep our focus for now, Morix, and concentrate on this layout and SAR plans for the crews. The dreadnought *Ambari* might be best for leading the fleet operations. If we split the Hygran patrol into three parts, we can cover more ground and have faster response times."

Morix29 nodded slowly and took a sip of her orange juice, going over the plans in her neutral network. UIPEs were not fixed physical entities, but in fact a series of highly-advanced algorithms and sentient software collections that used any and all available hardware to sustain themselves. They could exist just about anywhere and could utilise their vast data-banks and hyperfast info-net connections to come up with just about any solution to any problem.

Alanar wondered why she took so long to play it out in her mind.

"Commodore," she said eventually, "your idea for the Hygran ships is a very sound tactical idea, but I can't help but wonder why you're using that dreadnought for a flagship when there are three swordships available."

"This is a Hygran colony with Hygran ships on patrol. The Navy presence is assistance and immobile protection only. If I run this from a Confederation ship, it won't send a good message to the Directorate fleet. We need to work together."

A hologram flared between them of the Second Hygra system with crosses marking the Hygran forces and the Confederation protection force over the colony. A red circle surrounded Hygra and the dreadnought.

"As Commodore you will be responsible for three main objectives. One: the protection of Hygra. Two: the assistance of the Tardig and Winn Winn craft. Three: the running of Hygran perimeter patrols. You'll have to divide your time between all these and need to make your presence felt, which means travelling between these two points."

The circles flashed and oscillated briefly.

"To save time, why not split your time between two flagships? That way everyone gets catered for. As much as possible, anyway."

Alanar looked at the UIPE and smirked.

"You really have been in the business a long time, haven't you?

*   *   *

Nearly three hours later, the Commodore found himself making his way carefully through the corridors to the rigging that held the *Vigilant Watchman*. He had decided that if he couldn't make a swordship his permanent headquarters, he could at least depart Hygra on one. He'd never witnessed a take-off from underwater before – not first-hand, anyway.

Morix29 had secreted herself inside the networked linkages of the starship a half hour ago with some trepidation at sharing quarters with the 'stuffy' artificial intelligence that assisted the crew in its functions. This had left him a small amount of time to have his away kit transferred over and make a few arrangements. That included finding quarters on both the *Vigilant* and the *Ambari* which proved difficult in the case of the latter. Dreadnoughts were designed sparingly so they could be easily mass produced in the Founder's War which was probably why so few had survived the great conflict. He managed to find a place sharing with the Ship-Commander which had been a little awkward but necessary.

He came to one of the connection tubules joining the ship to the complex. The *Vigilant's* Talan Captain, Lal-ne-vo, and its Kin-Sai Flight Operations Officer were waiting there dutifully. Lal-ne-vo stood on its hind legs, a difficult balancing act for any insectoid hermaphrodite to perform, top most right arm striking a salute.

"At ease, Captain," Alanar said, smiling, but returning the salute. "You look like you might fall over."

"Of course, Commodore," the Talan clacked and buzzed before dropping to all sixes. "Please follow me."

Alanar tried hard to keep pace with the Captain as he was led through corridors, up ramps and up a ladder to the command, communication and control centre or C3C, the brain of the starship. Like every other aspect of the interior, it was a graceful blend of elegance and functionality. Ahead of him, at the other side of the room, were three huge screens displaying ship status, a real-time link to the view ahead of the ship and a 3-D representation of the surrounding space from left to right respectively.

Before the screens were two pilots inside gel-filled sensory deprivation suits that connected them directly to the vessels manoeuvring and guidance controls with no distractions. Three metres behind was a trio of podiums in a row: Shipboard Weapons, Command and Flight Ops. Further behind them were podiums and stations for the other department officers: Sensor Analysis, Communications and Engineering Liaison.

Everything, bar Marine operations and medical, were located in other areas of the ship. All were manned by a multitude of species: lots of Humans, but also Talans, Kin-Sai, Hygran and Centaurian. A venerable cross-section of the Confederation. There were a few exceptions, but generally speaking this was a similar scene on every Navy ship around the Galaxy.

Lal-ne-vo and his second-in-command occupied their respective podiums, Alanar standing to the left of command.

"With your permission, Commodore, we are ready to depart," the Talan reported, tapping several keys.

"Signal all ships and order them to depart. Then rendezvous at Hygar Moon with the Hygran taskforce," the Commodore ordered.

The Human communications officer acknowledged the order instantly, relaying it to the other Confederation ships.

"All departments report status and begin departure procedures," Lal-ne-vo began. "Command online and connected."

"Flight operations online. Support craft secure and standing by."

"Shipboard weapons online. Weapons and ordnance secured and on standby."

"Piloting and navigation online. All connections one hundred percent. Course laid in."

"Engineering online. Engines powering up to one hundred percent capability. SLIDE drive cycling up."

"Sensor analysis online. Network linkages established. Software at ready – steady."

"Communications online. Systems connected. Traffic Control has cleared our flight path."

Voices could now be heard over the PA system.

"Medical online. All crew implants show everyone five by five."

"Marine operations online. Suited up and ready to go."

There was a brief pause.

"AI?" Asked the Captain, tentatively.

The far-right main screen was briefly laced with static as two images tried to overlay each other before it split in two: Morix29 on the left, the featureless mannequin-like visage of the swordship, AI on the right.

"Online. Connections established and operating within parameters," they both said in unison before Morix29 shot her counterpart a filthy look.

The Captain and Commodore exchanged looks. This would be interesting.

"Detach primary umbilicals."

"Ports sealed. Umbilicals withdrawing.

"Begin separating the rigging."

"Opening rig. Primary umbilicals clear.

"Detach secondary umbilicals."

"Rigging and secondaries clear. We are drifting free now."

"Begin ascent."

Slowly the huge starship, two others like it and six shield-shaped counterparts a third of the size began moving up out of the base together. They quickly picked up speed and just as light from the base was leaving their lower hulls, light from the surface reached down to the topside. The glittering forms sent little of the local wildlife scattering. They were used to this kind of thing. Some bold ones even chased or attempted to attach themselves to the craft.

Vigilant was first to break the surface, its great form displacing millions of tonnes of water, sending spray flying in all directions. Even as it ascended out of the mist, another swordship began emerging. And a shieldship. Then another. And another. To all watching, it looked like a new chain of floating islands was emerging near the Hygran capital city. But these islands were malcontents, wishing to belong to the sky and space, not the sea.

So they kept rising, creating a small rain storm as water sluiced off their armour. A kilometre into their journey, out of the depths, all liquid had been removed and the mighty vessels began to assume standard Confederation fleet formation: shieldships forming a perimeter around the swordships. It took a further two kilometres to complete.

"We are in formation, Commodore," reported Morix29.

"Very good. All ships' armour secured?" Alanar asked.

"Yes, Commodore. We are clear to breach the atmosphere."

He looked at the view from the central screen, at the sprawling metropolis and hinterland before the Confederation ships. It would be the last time he saw Hygra for a while, so he tried to gather as much of it as he could in that small moment.

"Cease horizontal ascent. Head through the atmosphere to the rendezvous point. All ahead full."

"All ahead full, Commodore."

The small fleet began tilting upwards to forty-five degrees and increased its speed. The ships were still using gravatic drives and thrusters; igniting main engines this far inside the atmosphere could damage the environment irreparably over time. Outside the blue sky began to give way to black as space replaced atmosphere. Still the nine craft tilted through forty-five to sixty, then seventy.

"Clearing fusion exclusion zone in fifteen seconds," reported Morix. "Tilt is eighty-five percent complete."

"Ignite main drives the moment we clear the zone. Let's not keep our friends waiting."

In only a few seconds the ships became vertical. Artificial gravity had become active an hour before the departure so the transition was seamless. Any first-time cadet at a window might still have thrown-up from the disorientation. Alanar's training, combined with his synth-sym's efforts, prevented this from happening to him. Not that they were strictly needed. He was focused on the view ahead, distracted from any potential ill feelings.

Hygar Moon was not quite visible. It currently occupied a place on the night side. But there were other orbital facilities and parked ships to see. It was easy to forget that while they looked close, the objects were, in fact, nowhere near the Confederation Navy vessels. Few ships in the Galaxy would come out well from an encounter like that.

"We are clear. Main drives igniting."

From the 'hilt' engine sections of the swordships and three ports under the rear areas of the shieldships erupted dazzling trails of super-heated particles which sent them shooting away from the planet at high speed.

The ship status display was replaced by a 2-D view of the local space of Hygra, including the moon. A red line appeared from the fleet and curved round the orbit of Hygra to the moon where a red circle marked the Hygran contingent. Estimated time of arrival was only a few minutes.

"Status report, Captain," Alanar ordered, walking toward the real-time screen.

"All ship systems are green. The other craft are maintaining formation and report no damage."

"Get me a link to Ship-Commander Holon."

The wrinkled face of the dreadnought Ship-Commander's face appeared on the middle screen.

"Congratulations on a well-executed departure, Commodore."

"Thank you, Ship-Commander. We will be with you shortly. Are you ready for the jump?"

A hint of anxiety rippled across the old man's face.

"We are having some problems with one ship, Sir. But it's nothing that shouldn't be fixed upon rendezvous."

Alanar frowned, not liking the twinge of déjà vu he felt.

"Explain."

Holon took a deep breath through his nose and immediately confirmed Alanar's suspicions.

"One of our light-cruisers, the *Shamsha*, is reporting poor engine output and won't reach us until the same time you do. It's a common problem, Sir, especially with that vessel."

Navat! Bloody woman was doing this on purpose and for no reason other than she didn't like submitting to Confederation authority. He was going to have to keep an eye on her.

"Alright. As long as it's not a main drive issue, we can fix it later," the Commodore conceded, maintaining composure. "See you soon, Ship-Commander."

"Safe journey, Commodore."

The view returned to real-time forward, now dominated by Hygra and a slowly-emerging Hygar Moon.

"Continue on course. Captain, may Morix and I borrow your office?"

"Of course, Commodore. The AI will mark a route for you."

"Thank you." Alanar shot Morix a look and headed out of the C3C, following a path holographically laid out for him.

He quickly found the main captain's office which was used for general staff meetings, diplomatic talks and other, more mundane, activities. It was rather well-decorated by Talan standards: four Haxashle bushes, a water beaker and a few large organic-looking things Alanar didn't recognise. Thankfully, there was a desk and three chairs still there, or perhaps taken out of storage for him.

Morix appeared in front of him as he sat at the desk.

"Navat?" she asked.

"I wish you wouldn't do that. It's like you're Centaurian," he chided. "But, yes. I suppose I just want to vent, really."

"I could become more serious. Her record indicates a strong possibility of –"

"You looked into Hygran military service files?"

A small smirk graced the Hygran UIPE's face.

"I was…interested."

"How you managed it is what I want to know!"

"It's a common misconception amongst organics that UIPEs are essentially programmes operating in a system like you operate in the real world," she explained. "I am a system within the system. I can become it and be apart from it at the same time. There is no such thing as encryptions for me when it comes to the HDD. Now, shall we debate the ethics of that or shall we discuss Navat?"

Alanar couldn't help thinking that Navat wasn't the only one of his subordinates he should be concerned about.

"Alright, go on. But next time ask me first, please."

"As I said, there is a strong indication of insubordinate activity and dissention. Records show a history of headstrong behaviour and independence. That's fine on its own, but she's clearly irritated by Hydra's apparent lack of commitment amongst other things."

"Shit!" Alanar put his head in his hands and rubbed his temples. "Right, let's deal with this. I'll go over there and talk to her while we're en route."

"I recommend after the first jump. The media are raising enough questions about this."

He looked up.

"What are they saying?"

"Just asking about such a large deployment and questioning the cover story, as they do."

The Commodore quickly organised his thoughts with a little help from the synth-sym. The media was irrelevant to him. The PM and the Vice-Admiral would deal with them. Navat was his priority, as was getting the fleet to Second Hygra. Maintaining cohesion and the initiative were key to success.

"Alright, after the jump. Let's just get out of here."

He stood up and started to make his way out until something scuttled over his foot, nearly tripping him over. The Commodore looked down and frowned and then at Morix who smiled wryly.

"Kerensh Beetle," she said simply before flaring away.

He sighed, making his way out of the door into a corridor where he startled a passing Human male.

"Sorry," he quipped, still marching towards the C3C.

If this was what command was truly like, it was a miracle everyone above captain hadn't gone insane. Or maybe they had and concealed it very well.

The view from the forward real-time sensor showed the fleet had nearly arrived at the rendezvous. He could see Navat's craft limping along into formation with the other Hygran ships. It was a bit messy on the fleet display, but what could be done? He took a deep breath.

"Assume convoy formation one and prepare to cycle up the SLIDE."

The fleet began moving into a new pattern, a line of Confederation ships with the Hygrans escorting alongside. They began moving out away from the moon to clear the other traffic and stop any tracking attempts.

"We are aligned with Rally One," the AI reported.

"Cycle the jump drives and prepare for space-lane interface."

"Course laid in and cycling," said Morix.

"All ships are in formation and cycling," communications called.

"Begin the countdown."

"SLI in T-minus one minute."

"Are we still clear?"

"No tracking sensors are on us. Even the media has learned its place. We're good to go."

And so there was the slow wait for the countdown to end and the inter-dimensional flight through stringspace to begin.

Alanar had always enjoyed interstellar flight transitions. They were, as Humans liked to compare it, just like roller coaster rides without the G-forces. The Commodore had been to Sector Earth four years ago, tried one such amusement and couldn't help but agree, even if the mathematics behind such things escaped him.

"Gravatic manipulators online and deployed."

"Cycling complete."

"Ten seconds to interface."

A smile grew on his face as the fleet began bracing itself. He was jealous of the pilots the most. They must be experiencing such sweet anticipation.

"...two...one...interface!"

The spike-shaped gravatic manipulators focused on a single point several metres ahead of every ship in the fleet before diverging, ripping open holes in space itself. Inside the tears lay stringspace, a dimension full of strings linking every concentrated mass in the universe together. The more mass, the more strings and the easier it was to travel. And the more you travelled a string, the faster the transit became.

While Alanar had always struggled with the physics behind the transition technology, all Confederation citizens knew it was the same principle as how a rope made of many fibres was more useful than a single fibre. The key was finding the right string or set of strings and navigating them to their natural conclusion. Given they were essentially travelling to open space near the comet Rally One, that required a great deal of power and concentration.

Vigilant was latched onto by several strings and hauled into the dimensional chaos, followed shortly after by the rest of the fleet in the following nanoseconds. The masses of every craft instantly shrunk to zero, allowing them to travel at great speeds through the tangled mess.

Alanar watched the unfolding, seemingly endless, scene of multi-coloured strings whipping past the ships or shifting as they passed through the malaise. It seemed as though they were falling at the speed of light into nothingness due to the eerie green backlighting that appeared to lie beyond the strings. In all the centuries of stringspace travel, no-one had worked out what that glow was or why every sentient being who saw it got the impression they were falling towards it. Nor could anyone could explain the lack of a differential in time as ships transited.

The colours emanating from the screen played across the C3C, capturing the attention of all present. There really wasn't anything for anyone to do once stringspace had been entered, other than watch the pilots do their jobs. The AI maintained their suit connections to the ship and Engineering kept the power flowing. There was a certain security about that which you couldn't get in real-space.

Of course, you could fire weapons. But at such speeds, firing on a ship with no mass in an environment that had only one form of navigation, the damage would be light even if you could make a hit. No-one had ever won a battle there and no-one died in the transit ever. There were rumours from the Founder's War, but no-one could confirm much from when it was in its darkest days.

Morix was the only one who looked remotely bored by the experience apart from the AI, but it didn't have a face to look bored with. She'd had nearly two centuries of this, though maybe more outside of her service to the Confederation Navy. Perhaps it was possible to become bored with such things after a certain length of time.

"Transition thirty percent complete," reported the AI. "All ships are still with us."

It might not have looked bored, but it certainly sounded it.

Pulling himself away from the sight of the transit, Alanar reviewed the route the fleet had to take. The first jump would take it to Rally One, the code name for a comet that was the first marker on the military route to Second Hygra. Then they would transit to the Hak'na'krena, the name of a huge radiation storm that had collided with a brown dwarf remnant to create a firestorm dangerous to all but military grade starships.

After this it would be a final jump to the Second Hygra star system, behind the largest moon of the planet, to inform the Colony-Governor of their presence. It all sounded so easy, but in the meantime there were rest breaks needed for the pilots and system checks to do. Running a fleet was nowhere near as easy as it appeared. Which reminded him...

"Flight Officer Mwargh Argh," he literally barked to pronounce the Kin-Sai's name. "Please prepare a gunship to escort me to the *Shamsha*."

The massive hulk of a Flight Officer merely nodded in compliance. It was a running joke in the Navy that there weren't many Kin-Sai captains or admirals because they would terrify their subordinates with their naturally brutish manner and roaring vocalisations. It wasn't true, of course. Not all of them were so gruff and a great deal of their military officers were absorbed by the Battlefleet, unlike most of the Founder races. Still, it never hurt to poke fun. The Kin-Sai certainly did the same to Navy staff.

"Communications," he ordered. "When we emerge from stringspace, send a message to the *Shamsha* informing them of my intentions. Morix, I'd like you to run a fleet battle simulation between the Hygran ships. Navy vessels will run drills in the event of a perimeter breach. We jump out in two hours. Clear?"

"Yes, Commodore."

He smiled, moving to stand next to the command podium. The Captain glanced briefly at him, then turned once he realised the superior officer wanted something.

"Commodore?" it clacked.

"Captain, I wonder if you might join me in the spirit of co-operation."

The Talan's antennae twitched. Mild amusement, perhaps? Had the Talan picked up on the brewing conflict between the two parties as well?

"Certainly, Commodore," Lal-ne-vo agreed, shooting a look at the Flight Officer who gave another customary nod.

Alanar wondered how true the joke about the Kin-Sai would prove.

"Excellent. Walk with me."

The pair walked out of the C3C and began making their way down to the main launch landing bay. Despite causing it to walk awkwardly, the insectoid hermaphrodite maintained an upright gait.

"Captain, although you're on duty and need my permission, please consider this a blanket order to walk however you wish as long as I'm in command."

Lal-ne-vo bowed its head in appreciation and then dropped down.

"Thank you, Commodore. The Vice-Admiral and I have a similar arrangement, but I wasn't sure."

"Don't worry. I might have been given a snap promotion, but there will not be any power trips."

They climbed down a ladder between three decks.

"Our visit to the *Shamsha* has, I assume, something to do with that statement?"

"Is it that obvious?"

"Ship-Commander Navat is known for being difficult in Confederation-Hygran affairs."

The Commodore sighed heavily and jumped off the last rung.

"I thought nationalism died with the Founding?"

"Such things are rarely that simple. Navat is something of a mystery to me. The reasons for such feelings are not obvious."

Alanar felt he might have to defer to Lal-ne-vo on more issues as this mission progressed.

"Let's try and get her talking," he suggested firmly. "It usually helps."

"Transition eighty percent complete. Interface termination in three minutes," the AI's dull voice droned. "All hands prepare to re-enter normal space."

Why did AIs have to sound so bored all the time, the Hygran wondered. He was sure they could be made to sound more interesting, like some people did with house AIs. Then again, it might be inappropriate to do so if his command was only temporary.

A scaled-down version of Morix flared into existence to sit on his shoulder, making him jump slightly.

"May I suggest a fighter escort for your gunship as well, Commodore?"

It was then he noticed her ultraviolet colouring.

"Why are you—?" he asked quietly and sharply.

"Talans can't see the UV spectrum. It's a bit like dogs on Earth and some colours. Or Kin-Sai for that matter," the UIPE answered in that same bright tone. "I didn't wish to startle the good Captain. Use your implants to datavise me, too. I'm sure you don't want them to think you're crazy."

Alanar activated this synth-sym mailing systems and established a connection to her.

"Next time, ping me, please. And why would I need an escort to visit one of my own ships?"

"A little show of force never hurt anyone. If not a personal escort, may I at least recommend a combat air patrol around the fleet?"

He thought for a moment.

"Hmm, make it both. Set up a joint CAP and run it out of the dreadnought. See if you can't iron out any kinks before we hit Second Hygra. Two fighters will be fine as an escort."

Morix crossed her arms and looked dubious.

"I felt a full squadron might be appropriate and, of course, the Marines to go with it."

"You really don't like her, do you?"

"When you've been around as long as I have, Commodore, you learn that you can't like everybody. Especially not idiots."

He suppressed a laugh but not a small smile.

"That's my staff you're talking about."

"I stand by what I said."

"Just follow my orders, please, and don't start a war while I'm gone."

The UIPE merely nodded and zapped out of sight, severing the messenger connection. For all her rudeness, she was essentially right. However, the Commodore felt a much greater confidence regarding his role now. The various elements worked, yes, but as a fleet and a team they needed a focal, co-ordinating point.

The Captain and Commodore entered the main L-L bay through a wide door guarded by two Marines. Inside, in various rack and docking cradles, were the bulk of *Vigilant*'s massive compliment of crescent-shaped fighters and wasp-profiled gunships. There were literally hundreds of them, all readying for deployment.

Currently, their sleek, shiny hulls betrayed not even a hint of weaponry, but at the touch of a button the seemingly harmless craft could annihilate entire sections of cities.

Overhead, a series of mechanisms assisted in lowering two fighters and a gunship onto the deck plating where they were immediately set upon by flight control and operations personnel. A pair of Marines rushed up to flank them, their extremely slender, stick insectile figures betraying Talan origin. Not a full squadron, just enough for a casual honour guard.

"Transition complete. Disengaging interface and entering normal space," the AI announced flatly.

Alanar could imagine the fleet bursting out of stringspace in what was, hopefully, flawless convoy formation. Morix would be dispatching orders and information now and it would separate into groups in minutes, launching fighters and engaging in combat drills. Though the trip through stringspace had seemed to take a few minutes, hours had passed on the outside. They were well into the mission now.

A ramp unfolded from one side of the gunship as a side door slid away to reveal a spacious interior for sitting and standing. Gunships were designed to be able to hold up to two squads of Marines and carry a support vehicle on its undercarriage, so naturally there was more than enough room. The four people climbed inside while two Human pilots leapt into the cockpit. The Commodore uplinked to the lead pilot via his synth-sym as the craft began sealing up.

"Pilot, how are we progressing?"

"Just waiting for a return signal from *Shamsha*, then we can make our way over."

"Just go now. It'll be good to see the fleet in action."

"Yes, Commodore. Confirming with FCO. Launching now."

Below the three support ships the deck opened up and they shot out, initially on thrusters then switching too main drives, leaving trails of exhaust behind them.

Alanar looked out the windows at the ever-expanding view of the fleet with the giant comet Rally One providing a magnificent eerie blue-white background to it all. Other fighters were beginning to take flight now, followed by their supporting gunships. In addition to the Confederation Navy vessels, the Hygrans were flying their own v-shaped fighter-bombers and bulky shuttle-boats. The mixture of ships and the trails their engines left was truly awe-inspiring.

"What was the name of the dreadnought, Commodore?" asked Lal-ne-vo, staring at the Hygran warship.

"The *Ambari*."

"It wears its age well," the Talan commended, "but I'm still surprised to see one in a modern fighting force."

"I suppose the Hygrans only really needed a police force. They're too far inside the border to need anything heavy. And even if they weren't, who's going to attack them? The Tardigs?" Alanar laughed.

It was true. Despite the Tardig's over-zealous stance against the Winn Winn, they did share a very close relationship with the Confederation and had since they saved it from a war with the former Winn Winn Empire by declaring war on them first. While not the best solution to the problem, the brilliant leadership, innovative tactics and incredible efficiency of the Republic military had probably saved more lives and done less damage than a fight between the Navy and Winn Winn would have.

The gunship tore towards the old dreadnought, once the pinnacle of military technology in the old Empire. Centuries ago, thousands of the monsters had roamed the space of the now defunct Centaurian Empire, first working together to protect the colonies and maintain order, then fighting brutally to control them in the Founder's War.

Now there were only perhaps two hundred left, the others victims of the war, scrapped or destroyed in various accidents or incidents since. It was a shame. Each craft had its own unique and colourful history, especially from the war. He made a mental note to check the *Ambari's* own when he got back.

The trio of Navy ships looped under and around the warship before lining up with the light cruiser. *Shamsha* looked even more foreboding than the other ships in the joint fleet. Its bay doors gaped open like a giant maw, preparing to swallow up the three craft whole. Alanar braced himself as they landed. This disciplinary would not be pretty, he felt.

The doors unlocked and slid back to reveal no honour guard waiting for them.

"What a surprise," Alanar breathed quietly as he climbed out onto the deck. No-one was waiting for them at all, in fact.

He glanced at Lal-ne-vo, tramping around the other side on all sixes, looking suitably unimpressed.

"I suppose we should make our way to the C3C," suggested the Captain. "I do hope you are still confident about this mission, Commodore, because this kind of insubordination escapes me."

Alanar shook his head wearily.

"I'm afraid I can't afford that kind of cynicism, Captain."

"Sorry, Sir."

"Oh no, Captain, it's fine. I just wish it wasn't so."

The Hygran motioned for the Marines to wait where they were and began walking towards the exit of the bay, his Talan captain following just behind.

Initially, Alanar had been tempted to fly into a rage over this kind of insolence, but he realised that it would accomplish very little. Talking and warning calmly was the solution.

They strolled towards the gravlift at the end of one of the corridors. Unlike Confederation Navy ships, Hygran craft tended to rely on very hi-tech ways of moving about their interiors. There were no ramps, few ladders and narrower corridors, allowing for more compact design but posing more of a safety hazard in emergencies.

Once the pair stepped inside the cylindrical room, a door closed behind them and a holographic map of the ship appeared between them.

"Please select a destination," a mechanistic voice requested.

Alanar peered at the design intently. Whatever size they were, starships were always nearly universally complicated. Hygran light-cruisers were little different in that regard. He found himself missing Morix's help, no matter how unwarranted it usually was. He spotted the target.

"Deck five!" he ordered and the hologram vanished, followed by a quiet whirring noise as the lift shot upward.

"If the Hygrans end up getting into a fight with any of the combatants they'd better act fast," noted Lal-ne-vo looking about the lift. "One well-placed shot could cripple the internal workings of this ship."

"I really hope it won't come to that, Captain. I'd prefer not to oversee a firefight with the Tardigs or the Winn Winn."

"Not to sound arrogant, Commodore, but I doubt *we* would have much trouble in a one-on-one battle with either side's craft."

The Commodore smirked.

"That's not arrogance, Captain. It's the security that comes from commanding a swordship that can destroy a small flotilla."

The antennae twitched. Just a little.

The doors opened and the pair stepped out, moving towards the main entrance of the C3C, guarded by four Defence Directorate guardsmen. All of them focused on the two Confederation Navy officers as they approached.

"Good afternoon, gentlemen – and lady," Alanar added quickly, noting the female guard, and moving to walk past them.

The closest Hygran placed himself between Alanar and the doorway.

"Sorry, Sir, this is a restricted area," he said, putting up a hand.

"I'm the Commodore of this fleet, Ship-Guardsman. Nowhere is off limits to me."

"The Ship-Commander's permission is required before entering sensitive ship areas for all non-crew members."

Perhaps flying into a rage might have been the better approach.

"In that case, could you contact the Ship-Commander and request permission, please?"

"Yes, Sir," the ship-guardsman said, putting a hand to his headset and turning away.

Evidently the crew had been instructed to be as obstructive as possible, or Navat had decided to use them as pawns in whatever game she was playing. If the former was the case he couldn't replace her without serious ructions. If the latter was true, then undoubtedly she had considered ways of manipulating them out of office. Bloody hell, why couldn't she just co-operate?

The ship-guardsman turned round again, the door opening as he did so.

"Go ahead, Sir."

Alanar resisted the urge to glare at the ship-guardsman and stepped forward into the Hygran C3C.

"Ship-Commander Navat," he said loudly, trying not to betray any annoyance. "You received my message – yes?"

The woman turned slowly from her place before the single huge screen showing the tactical view of the local area with a specific focus on the *Vigilant*.

"I did indeed, Commodore Alanar. Though what exactly this visit is all about I am not so clear on," she said, walking towards them, smiling falsely.

They met in the middle of the C3C, nearly nose to nose.

"Spot inspections to improve cohesion," he explained, also smiling falsely. "Captain Lal-ne-vo is here to observe and share ideas. You're also invited aboard the *Vigilant Watchman*, though I see you already have an eye on it."

"A standard tactical assessment, Commodore. As you may have noticed, though, I have something of a situation on my hands and a tour might not be too convenient currently."

"A meeting in your office, then. I know I could do with a glass of Ferex juice."

The engagement was over and he had won.

"Of course," she conceded. "Please follow me. Ship-Assistant Laxix, you have the command."

She led them off the deck and down another corridor to her private office and quarters. On the way Alanar noticed a great deal of Hygran artwork and ornamentation. It was beautiful, but he questioned its place on a military vessel.
Eventually, they reached the office and entered in utter silence. The place was incredibly clean and organised, but with the same Hygran cultural pieces, including a very impressive sculpture of Hygra and its moon suspended in an AG field.

"Please sit," said Navat. "Captain Lal-ne-vo, can I get you anything?"

"Hish Root, if you have any," replied the Talan, perching itself on the chair awkwardly.

"I'm afraid I only stock Hygran cuisine and beverages in my office, Captain. Perhaps Ferex juice might put you in better stead?" she said, pouring herself and Alanar a glass of thick orange-coloured liquid, pulling out a third from her desk in readiness.

Lal-ne-vo's antennae twitched again in amusement.

"I'll go without, Ship-Commander. Ferex doesn't have the best effects on my species' biology."

"Really?" She said with false incredulity.

"It's similar to the effect alcohol has on Hygrans."

The Ship-Commander's eyes widened and a smirk pricked her face for a moment.

"Right, Ship-Commander," began Alanar, taking a sip of the Ferex, "I think it's important we get to the point as diplomatically as possible. Obviously, this isn't an inspection, but it is related to unit cohesion. Your attitude since this mission began has been incredibly disruptive, obstructive and insubordinate. This ship is a vital component to our mission and I need my team working to full capacity. So, would you care to explain what is going on and maybe we can find a solution?"

Navat smiled, sighed, stood and walked to the AG sculpture.

"Ship-Commander?" asked the Commodore more sternly.

"Do you know how many of our people died when the Centaurians invaded and occupied our world, Commodore?" the woman asked. "How many civilians? Families?"

Alanar sighed. Despite being centuries ago, the scars left by the Founder's War were obviously still there for some in the Confederation. In their drive to find cannon fodder to use in their civil war, the Centaurian Empire had come to Hygra with a fleet of dreadnoughts. What followed was one of the more regrettable actions of an already shameful conflict: a brutal and overwhelming invasion of yet another world.

"Too many," he admitted carefully, playing out the painful scene in his head. "Far, far too many."

"It was seventy-two million. Men, women and children. Old and young. Healthy and crippled," Navat said quietly, tapping a few buttons on the sculpture.

In seconds, Hygra transformed from a healthy living world to a cratered, grey burning mess. Its moon, too, showed signs of extensive orbital bombardment and damage.

"No-one knows still how many more were maimed, tortured and experimented on when the Centaurian scientists arrived. And then there were those they sent to fight for them. I don't think anyone even bothers to try and guess anymore." Then she added, "And it was all for absolutely nothing."

At this point Lal-ne-vo intervened.

"With respect, that isn't true, Ship-Commander," said Lal-n-vo in what should have been a strong tone, but had clearly been filtered out to sound less confrontational. "While millions of people died from all the Founder species, billions more lived to see the Confederation."

The Hygran female snorted, waving her hands dismissively.

"Tell me, Captain. Given the vast numbers the conquest of Humanity gave to the Empire, do you really think our species' had to suffer such catastrophic losses in order to live the way we do now? The Confederation does not reimburse us for the slaughter inflicted on us. It merely legitimises it now – falsely."

Alanar struggled to keep his cool.

"Ship-Commander, I hope you aren't suggesting that our contribution in the Founder's War was pointless."

"Indeed I am, Commodore," she replied, making her way back to her seat, the AG sculpture still glowing with false nuclear fires and devastation. "The discovery of Humanity a little sooner would have saved Hygra and countless of other worlds from the Centaurian yoke. I, unlike the rest of the Galaxy, refuse to forget all those who died needlessly in that war. Free Hygra recognises the hypocrisy of the Confederation for what it is."

The Talan and male Hygran exchanged brief but worried glances. Despite the centuries, generations and widespread reconciliation, for some the wounds of the Founder's War would never heal. Free Hygra was just one of several movements across the Founder worlds that saw the Confederation not as a beacon of freedom and equality, but as a cancer on their worlds; a new legitimised form of the Empire and now extinct Rebellion factions of old.

Usually, their influence didn't reach such positions in the Confederation or the fleets of the Founder species and so the potential for conflict was minimal. But here Alanar was in this exact position. If he didn't deal with this exactly right who knew what might happen.

"Whether or not the Confederation is built to cover the slaughter of millions or not, Ship-Commander, the fact is that you are deliberately hindering a military expedition of vital importance. If this were war time I could have you removed from your command," Alanar threatened.

"You'd be welcome to try, Commodore. But my ship, though small, is loyal to me and Hygra in its entirety," Navat interjected calmly.

"However," Alanar continued, "this is not war time and so we can come to a more amicable agreement. The last thing I want is any mutual hostility between us."

The Ship-Commander gave a small nod.

"I'll assign this ship its own patrol route and mission in the Second Hygra system. As projections are that combat is unlikely, you will have little need to interact with Navy or other HDD personnel, thus avoiding any potential incidents. In an emergency, though, I expect you to follow the orders of myself or my officers."

"That is...acceptable."

The concession appeared to have worked, but only time would tell exactly how successful it was going to be.

"And until we reach Second Hygra?" Navat continued.

"Keep your convoy position. Morix will limit your role in all fleet exercises en route."

She nodded again and stood.

"If that is all, Commodore, Captain, I have a ship to run."

The Confederation Navy officers stood. Lal-ne-vo saluted Navat out of respect, a gesture not returned by Navat nor displayed to Alanar who broke the tension by turning and walking toward the door in silence, the Talan following closely behind. The pair remained quiet for the entire trip back to the gunship, Lal-ne-vo appreciating that his superior was deep in thought and requiring time to work out his next move.

Alanar's mind was a storm of thought and ideas. He was effectively one ship down already in the first leg of his mission and couldn't help but wonder how this concession would affect his standing in the fleet, particularly with the Hygran contingent. How could Morix not have known about Navat's Free Hygra connection? Damn Navat for keeping it so well hidden.

They entered the launch-landing bay and climbed aboard the gunship, the two Marines taking in the Commodore's stern face and joining Lal-ne-vo in silence. Shortly after launching the Captain dared to break the silence.
"If I may, Commodore...?" it broached cautiously.

"You may, Captain. It would be a welcome distraction."

"Your decision about Navat was admirable. I do hope you are not doubting yourself."

Alanar smiled.

"Of course not, Captain. But thank you nonetheless."

"I cannot imagine the distress she must feel. Talan'klee was also heavily damaged in the war, but I feel no venom for the Confederation."

The Hygran leaned forward a little, rubbing his temples.

"It's all about perspective, I suppose. But I see little to be gained from her viewpoint and the war is over and has been for so long."

"She seemed particularly loathing of the Centaurians and Humans," the Talan noted. "I can understand the former but not the latter."

The Commodore shook his head slowly as he went over his knowledge of the Founder's War.

"The Humans did some pretty terrible things in the war as I understand, especially towards its end when the rebels assaulted Hygra. They even saw action at Talan'klee when there was an uprising shortly before the ceasefire conference," Alanar explained. "Still, it's not like they didn't suffer as a species, too. The Earth today is not what it was pre-conquest. Neither is the Human species, so I'm told."

"I would imagine that would be more of a reason to support the Confederation to prevent that kind of disaster occurring again."

Alanar resisted the urge to explain it away as Navat just being an ignoramus, despite his frustration.

"I agree, but you can't impress that view on someone from Free Hygra. Their argument talks past ours. Hopefully, my solution will keep her out of my hair until we get back to Hygra."

Lal-ne-vo's antennae twitched in amusement.

"I think you spend far too much time in the company of Humans, Commodore."

"How so?"

"You have no hair."

The Hygran laughed, rekindling his good mood. Maybe this mission could be more than just seriousness and sparring with insubordinate officers. Command was supposed to be enjoyed. Navat would not bring him down.

He watched as the gunship tore past one of the swordships, reading the lettering printed along one side. It was Captain Shuresh's *Star Dragon*, the oldest Confederation craft in the fleet at about two hundred years old. The ship had picked up a great deal of character in that time with various designs stencilled on its armour by each of its captains and a few minor add-ons and modifications.

Strictly speaking, such things weren't proper military protocol, but the Navy allowed it on the condition it wasn't interfering with regular functioning. More regimented species and societies avoided it stiffly but some, like the Humans and Fale, enjoyed decorating their craft in various ways. Despite his own species' preference for formality and order, Alanar liked the untidiness. He gave serious thought to taking a tour after the next jump.

"Pilot!" he called, hitting an intercom button. "Take the scenic route."

He looked at Lal-ne-vo and smiled.

"We have time to kill," he said jovially. "Let's see our fleet in action."

The small wasp-profiled ship broke off from its trajectory toward the *Vigilant* and flew out towards the perimeter, Rally One lighting up the area all around. It then began a slow loop around the fleet to observe what was taking place.

All the Hygran craft were performing battle manoeuvres against each other while the Confederation vessels maintained convoy formation, silently running drills to test reaction times. It made for interesting viewing, even when no activity was perceived. Even in this day and age, with so much space travel and star-flight occurring, the vastness of the vacuum made common viewing of ship-to-ship actions rare. Few appreciated the vastness of whole planets and moons, much less the massive volume that was Confederation space, or even the galaxy as a whole. Alanar, like many he supposed, tried not to think about it in depth. Size could still leave you feeling agoraphobic.

The gunship and its escorts completed the loop and banked inward, towards the *Vigilant Watchman*.

"I imagine the next jump will be less spectacular," commented Lal-ne-vo.

"Well, the Hak'na'krena isn't renowned as a sightseeing destination exactly," admitted Alanar. That and he didn't want to risk losing ships in that hellish locale.

"How confident are you about the *Vigilant*'s ability to fast-jump?" he asked tentatively.

The Talan thought for a moment.

"Navy ships are built to survive at least two consecutive fast-jumps with minimal damage, but I cannot guarantee the fleet would all wind up in the same area in Second Hygra."

The Commodore looked at the space outside, considering the ships he could still see.

"If we fast-jumped to Second Hygra it might cut a large chunk of our transit time."

"The Hygrans might not like that."

"They might not like the Hak'na'krena so much either."

The Talan stayed silent this time. The very reason the radiation super storm was on the military route to Second Hygra and not the regular one was because it could only be navigated by craft with military grade protection. Of course, what constituted military grade varied from species to species, planet to planet, and not all stood up to the same punishment Navy ships did.

"I suppose we could try and skirt the edge of it, Commodore," Lal-ne-vo piped up eventually as the gunship and its escorts came in to land. "But again it might not be an achievable manoeuvre for the Hygran craft."

"Hmm," was Alanar's only comment before the craft landed softly on the deck plating.

The doors slid back once more and this time Alanar was greeted by an honour guard of ten Marines, Morix29 and the two pilots of the escort fighters. The UIPE winked quickly at him as he walked towards the group.

"I know you weren't gone long, but a Commodore should always have an honour guard," she explained, a small smile briefly gracing her digital features.

"You know me too well," Alanar replied, drawing level with her. "Walk with me, please."

"I take it your 'inspection' met with some success?"

The three walked in a line towards the exit. Morix transmitted a dismissal order to the honour guard. The Commodore gave Lal-ne-vo a dubious look before answering.

"I would prefer the term 'limited' success, Morix, but at least we have a solution that ensures there won't be a shooting match – literally anyway."

Morix29 nodded.

"What did you offer her?"

"Independent operational status, except in emergencies."

Her eyes widened briefly.

"I know it's a lot, but there weren't any really favourable alternatives."

"The stockade?"

"Navat commands great loyalty in her crew," Lal-ne-vo explained. "Military prison would only exacerbate the situation."

"Makes sense. She is very much a love or loathe person. Almost makes you wish the Empire was still around."

The Commodore laughed.

"Please don't say that in front of Navat or she'll start a mutiny."

They stopped to let a group of crewmen carrying kinetic slam round cases to a loading bay get past.

"Well, at least then we would have had an easy way of resolving the problem," the UIPE noted, eyeing up the ammunition as they passed through her form.

"Hmm, don't tempt me."

They continued, walking toward the command centre.

"By the way, I'd like a capability report on all the Hygran craft," Alanar requested firmly.

"Of course, Commodore," Morix29 agreed. "Anything in particular?"

"Yes. Check their armour's heat and radiation resistance and their fast-jump abilities. Preferably in the next few minutes, please."

The UIPE simply smiled and flared away.

"Captain, I need to borrow your office."

"Not a problem, Commodore."

"In the meantime, keep things ticking over here. We could be seeing Second Hygra sooner than expected."

Lal-ne-vo bowed and scuttled off, leaving the Hygran alone to make his way to the leafy office. The vessel was quite quiet for a ship on manoeuvres and he met few crew members on his way. Not necessarily a bad thing, though. It meant everything was where it should be, everyone was at their stations and he could get to the office faster.

He entered to find a beetle buzzing around the console. He quickly waved the insect away before sitting down and sighing loudly. If this was what admirals had to put up with on a daily basis then he was glad this assignment was temporary.

Tapping a few keys on the keyboard he called up a fleet schematic and map of the local area, including the projected course to Second Hygra. In seconds he had a new course of fast-jumps laid in. A fast but incredibly risky way of reaching the objectives. He hoped Morix29 could give him a report that would make it possible for it to happen. If they could pull it off the Navy would be incredibly impressed, as would the casualties from the battle. It all depended on that report.

Another beetle scurried over the table top. How in Hygra did Lal-ne-vo get anything done in here, the Commodore wondered, nearly swatting it. He imagined his own quarters back in Hygra would be considered Spartan compared to this.

The console chirped as a subspace message was delivered to it. Accessing it, he discovered it was from Navy Command at Star Haven.

He breathed sharply, raising his eyebrows as he saw who exactly the message was from.

It was from none other than the Head of the Security and Intelligence Agency, Admiral Nukala Avec Chaven, perhaps one of the most powerful people in the Confederation. The SIA was the eyes and ears of the Navy within and outwith the borders, utilising a fleet of stalkerships and army of agents equipped with highly-advanced technology. It only sent messages containing the most important information.

Alanar pressed play and the image of the winged Centaurian sprang to life.

"Greetings, Commodore Alanar, and congratulations on your new position," the ridged face began, a synthetic voice relaying the words that were broadcast telepathically in person. "I was contacted by Vice-Admiral Suchovskaya shortly after you left, requesting any assistance my agency could render. Thankfully, we had several assets in the area at the time on hand to help. I've provided you with a data-package containing all we have been able to garner. If you require any further help, don't hesitate to get in touch. The situation out there is of great interest to Navy Command. Good luck, Commodore."

The alien saluted and the message ended.

Great, thought Alanar, just what I need – more pressure. He opened the data-package and began looking through it, paying close attention to the analysis of the combatant vessels. Two Tardig attack frigates and a strike-cruiser had engaged five Winn Winn warspheres that had been heavily modified. One of the frigates and two spheres had been destroyed before the Winn Winn had detonated a spatial concussion bomb, crippling all the survivors and releasing a huge shockwave.

He shook his head. Spatial concussion bombs were notoriously difficult to control. The Winn Winn were lucky not to have blown themselves away completely. They must have been desperate. Alanar could only imagine what had made them that way. Or indeed, how SIA had gotten such detailed information so fast. The people there were brilliant.

The Commodore forwarded the relevant data to the Confederation ship-commanders and allocated them the vessels to assist. The medical facilities available would be more than adequate to deal with the survivors, but at least three of the craft were damaged beyond repair, including the Tardig vessels. They would not be pleased about that.
Morix29 flared into existence before him in life-size form.

"I have compiled my report, Commodore."

"Very good. And...?"

"All the Navy ships have far superior capabilities to the Hygrans, of course, but surprisingly their ships are remarkably resistant to damage due to how they are built. Even the destroyers can hold up under intense solar radiation for an hour or so."

"And the fast-jumps?"

"I'm afraid the news there is less promising," she admitted. "The light-cruisers and two of the destroyers are relatively new and better equipped to deal with any feedback damage, but the other destroyers have suffered some wear and tear over the decades and that dreadnought is...'vintage' to say the least."

"They wouldn't survive the manoeuvre intact." Alanar sighed.

"Not currently, but with a few temporary modifications they could transit with minimal system loss. But it couldn't be for more than two jumps or they will end up way off course and disabled."

Alanar smiled.

"That's all we need. How long will the modifications take?"

"Under half an hour. They should be made aware of the risks, though."

"I'll get the Navy engineering teams on standby."

Morix29 nodded and a holomap of a star system appeared next to her, quickly zooming in on the fourth planet in the area. It was clearly verdant and fertile, and from the asteroid mine orbiting high above, inhabited.

"The Golden Horizon agricultural colony is not far from Second Hygra and, despite its status, is more equipped to deal with any emergency that arises."

Alanar peered at the map as it focused on the asteroid. It was highly developed on close inspection, appearing to be able to accommodate anything smaller than a shieldship. Though impressive, one had to wonder what agri-col was doing in possession of such a feat of engineering.

"There's also a Navy taskforce stationed there for planetary defence and border control. It could come in handy if things get desperate."

"Who's commanding?"

"Captain Benjamin Herkley, aboard the *Shining Hope*. You know each other?"

The Commodore shook his head.

"Not really. Hopefully he'll be co-operative if it comes to it. I wonder why they didn't send his taskforce instead of ours?"

"Golden Horizon has been experiencing some issues lately with criminal elements and the Navy probably doesn't want to be seen to throwing its weight around. Let's look at our objective."

The hologram melted away to be replaced by another of the Second Hygra system. Again it refocused on one of the planets, a huge gas giant banded with blues and purples. It was Muthavia, the biggest world in the system.

"Intelligence indicates that the battle-zone is over the Muthavia's north pole, though the fast-jumps probably shouldn't be aimed there," the UIPE continued.

"True. We don't want to end up causing a shipping accident," agreed Alanar. "We'll come out over one of the moons and approach from there. Go and make the modifications. We'll get the fleet into formation and get underway as soon as you are done."

"Yes, Commodore."

She, too, melted away with the Muthavia hologram, leaving Alanar alone to plan the fleet layout for Second Hygra. He called up the fleet status panel, accidentally pulling up the contents of Admiral Chaven's message. Before closing it he noticed something unusual when he glanced at the scans of the border. There appeared to be several very large movements of shipping on the border around Golden Horizon and Second Hygra.

This in itself was not atypical behaviour. Winn Winn space was still a warzone following the occupation by the Tardig military. However, there were no nearby systems on that side of the border. Indeed, it was one of the reasons the incursion had come as such a surprise. Of course, it could just be tightening of border security and extraction preparations, yet the number of ships involved was a bit overkill.

There must have been an entire fleet out there and not just any fleet, either. The scans showed several dozen super-capital-ships had entered the area – battlecarriers, battlecruisers and the feared megaships. Now, that was interesting. Why did they have their planet killers on border patrol? The Republic, despite its many commonalities with the Confederation, was incredibly militaristic compared to the other neighbouring civilisations and worlds in this area of the Galaxy, and known for its military proficiency. It rarely made deployments without following strict, sound military reasoning. He shook his head in futility. It was not his job to analyse Tardig military machinations, but it didn't make the situation any less confusing.

He returned to his previous goal, trying to ignore the report. Hopefully, it wouldn't matter too much given the speed at which the Confederation response was about to occur. With that in mind he began leafing through fleet operations guides for any useful information on how to proceed with the solution to this type of mission.

Even in this day and age, joint operations beyond patrol work were unusual. This was mostly due to the sheer lack of significant national navies, especially amongst the Founder races, a side effect of the Founder's War. Even the nations that joined the Confederation following the war did not possess firepower on a scale even approaching the Confederation Navy. There was just no need for it.

So the Commodore was left with only abstract theories and historical instances from decades past, none of which were particularly helpful. The last time the Navy had co-operated with the Member World militaries in actions like this was during the Na'thax Hive Swarm Crisis a century ago.

The keys to success seemed to lie in securing the system as fast as possible and isolating the combatants long enough for their pick up by the Republic or settlement in the Confederation. A simple enough task one would imagine, but doubtless there would be issues and he wanted to be ready for them.

Twenty minutes later he received a message calling him to the command centre from Morix29. Clearly they were ready.

Strolling onto the deck he found everyone in position and the display showing the fleet moving into formation.

"Modifications have been completed and the fleet will be ready to jump in three minutes," reported the UIPE.

"Excellent! Good work all of you. Communications, get me fleet-wide," Alanar ordered.

"You have fleet-wide, Commodore," said the Communications Officer after a few moments.

"This is Commodore Alanar to the fleet," the Hygran began. "Due to time constraints, amongst other concerns, I have decided to fast-jump the fleet to Second Hygra, specifically to the moon of Muthavia where individual fleet operations will begin. As I speak the new co-ordinates are being uploaded to your commanders. In mere moments we will be arriving at our objective. Thank you for your co-operation and I'll see you on the other side."

He nodded at the Communications Officer who terminated the link.

"SLIDE drive cycling up. Co-ordinators laid in," reported Lal-ne-vo.

"SLI in t-minus two minutes," the AI reported blandly. "Cycling is seventy percent complete."

"Preparing to run up reactors for fast jump."

Morix29 appeared next to him.

"I think the ship's AI thinks I'm cramping its style on screen," she declared huffily.

"Morix, it has no emotions or style to cramp."

She looked straight at him, an eyebrow raised.

"Commodore, with the greatest respect, you have much to learn about my kind and those like us."

He returned the look and folded his arms.

"You could still do worse than me."

"Hmm. Am I allowed to reserve judgement on that?"

He snorted quietly and looked back at the display screens. The formation was nearly completed and the jump process nearing its end. Anticipation was slowly building again, mixed in with a touch of concern about the fast-jumps.

"Cycling complete."

"All ships are in formation."

"SLI in thirty seconds."

Information continually flooded in about the ship, fleet, surrounding space and target spaces, even more than had come in before. Despite the simplicity of the actual fast-jump itself, the monitoring, planning and co-ordination behind it was demanding to the point of pushing limits, especially for the pilots. Every scrap of data was vital.

"Ten seconds."

Lal-ne-vo was glancing about at its crew, checking up on their progress and body language. Alanar imagined the other captains and ship-commanders were doing the same. He hoped he hadn't unnerved them completely with this decision.

"Five seconds."

But the decision had been made and he couldn't take it back now.

"Space-lane interface."

And so began the rollercoaster ride towards the Hak'na'krena that would mark the end of the second leg and beginning of the third leg of their journey. Using the new course co-ordinates, the fleet would enter a dense part of the storm for a brief few seconds then jump again to the target system. Once there the deployment and recovery from transit would begin, a process greatly slowed by the fast-jumps, but given the slash in interstellar travel time this would not pose as big a problem as it may have.

"Exiting stringspace."

The fleet emerged into a raging maelstrom of bright, shining yellows, red and blinding white beams. This was the beautiful, murderous reality of the Hak'na'krena, a storm of awe-inspiring ferocity that moved through the Galaxy at a slow, yet unstoppable pace. Its power had and would burn organic life from worlds and melt solid crusts out of existence. Here everything burned, even initially resistant starship armour.

"Transition complete."

"All ships accounted for."

"Commencing fast-jump cycling."

Alanar noticed that, in direct contrast to her reaction to her string space, Morix seemed transfixed by the sight of the deadly inferno before her. Its light beams seemed to sear through her holographic form in several places, completely concealing those parts before the filters adjusted and restored them.

"You know the Science Directorate predicted that eventually the Hak'nakrena will pass through the Hygran home system in forty million years," she said quietly, still not moving.

"I have the feeling by that time Hygra will be sufficiently prepared."

"Imagine how beautiful the sky will be."

"From behind a very big shield? I imagine quite beautiful indeed." She broke her gaze as the transit recommended.

"Sorry, Commodore. Even UIPEs can be distracted at times."

Alanar nodded as the next entry point opened and the burning space that was the Hak'nakrena disappeared before tears in space-time that the fleet quickly entered. The third leg had begun. And the moment it did a tremor ran through the deck beneath the Commodore's feet. Already the fast-jump transit was exerting a strain on the ship.

A strain that would only worsen as the SLIDE continued.

"Structural integrity field is fluctuating," reported the AI, loudly.

"Within acceptable tolerances," whispered Morix29, "and it's forgetting –"

"EM surges on the IBL dedicated areas."

The UIPE's eyes widened slightly.

"I hope the other ships aren't having such a bad time," Alanar commented as a stronger tremor rolled across the ship again. The left display screen flickered a little.

"I hate to say it, but this is moderate next to what the others are going through," she pointed out. "Power just failed on the forward observation lounge and the lower decks report fluctuations."

He looked right at her.

"I thought Navy craft were hardened against this kind of punishment?"

"They are, yes, but keep in mind we just passed through a radiation storm and stringspace is chaotic at the best of times," she replied. "We can handle it, though, so long as –"

"Deploying repair nanobots to affected areas."

"If it doesn't stop doing that I'm going to delete it one line of code at a time!"

Alanar looked about the C3C at the crew again. Clearly they were very agitated but performing well nonetheless. There was something to be said for Navy training, but he didn't like having to put them through that. Once this mission was over he'd ask the Vice-Admiral for fleet-wide shore leave on Second Hygra, for the pilots especially.

"Situation stabilising," declared the AI, "but the instability in the SI field remains."

"What can we do to correct it?" asked Lal-ne-vo.

"Not possible. Exposure of hull to stringspace makes mitigation unfeasible."

Morix29 flared away and into existence as her smaller form version on the Command console.

"If I may offer some reassurance, Captain, we are within acceptable tolerance levels. And our transit is over sixty percent complete."

The Talan regarded the tiny hologram for a moment.

"I appreciate the sentiment, Morix29, but I am still apprehensive. My ship has never been fast-jumped before."

"We will be fine, Captain. A little turbulence never hurt anyone."

Another tremor thrummed away as if to deliberately throw doubt on her words.

"You'll forgive me if I find that somewhat hard to believe."

She crossed her arms and gave a small smile, maintaining full confidence in herself and her words.

The next few minutes passed by relatively quickly and, almost thankfully in the case of many in the fleet, without major incident, until the ships finally began exiting the depths of stringspace one by one.

"Transition complete."

"Begin scanning the other ships and collect damage reports," ordered Alanar. "And start locating the objective craft."

The Commodore walked over to the left screen showing an ever-expanding view of the Second Hygra system. It appeared the entire fleet had survived the transit, but the formation was scattered and they weren't as close the Muthavian moon as he'd hoped.

"All ships reporting negligible or minor system damage apart from the *Ambari*."

Alanar looked at the Communications Officer, worry quickly crossing his face.

"What's wrong with the *Ambari*?

"They appear to have had blowouts on several decks. No casualties but their communications, sensors and weapons have all suffered damage."

He swore under his breath. "Do they require assistance?"

The Officer paused momentarily, checking with the ageing dreadnought.

"Ship-Commander Holon informs me it would be most appreciated."

The Hygran smiled. Doubtless that was not what Holon had said.

"Alright. Issue deployment orders to the rest of the fleet. I am transferring the flag to the *Ambari*. Morix, you're with me."

He turned to Lal-ne-vo.

"Captain, with your permission I'd like to take some engineering teams with me to assist repairs."

"As many as you need, Commodore. We'll keep you updated on our progress with the battle casualties."

"I'll take ten — and thank you."

He marched out of the C3C with Morix29 by his side, leaving the Talan and his Kin-Sai flight officer to glance at each other, shake their heads and get back to work. Walking towards the L-L bay at quick pace, the pair seemed to encounter half of the vast crew of the swordship as they prepared to receive the crew of their assigned vessel.

"I can only imagine the carnage when they start taking on the casualties," Alanar commented, taking in the sight.

"Once the Navy ships establish orbit around the colony you might get the chance. Especially once the Winn Winn learn there are Tardigs on the other ships. It'll be a security nightmare."

"Hmm," was the only sign of agreement as they entered the L-L Bay, also abuzz with activity.

The Commodore identified the engineering officer in the crowd and walked up to the female Human.

"Officer Anderson, are your teams ready to go?"

"Loading the last of the equipment now, Commodore. My gunship is posing a few problems," she replied quickly.

"You are coming with the contingent?"

"I am indeed. This is my crew and the Captain has signed off on it."

"I'm glad for your help, Officer. As no doubt will be the crew of the *Ambari*."

The woman smiled widely and climbed into the cabin of a gunship to secure some cargo. Alanar and the UIPE continued onwards to their own gunship.

"I meant to ask," the Hygran began. "The numbers in your name. Are there other Morixes out there?"

She flashed onto his shoulder, a smaller version dangling her legs off the edge.

"Oh no, Commodore," she laughed. "There is only one me. I don't think the Galaxy could handle any more."

"So...?"

"It's the last two digits of the year I was born. Among UIPEs it's something of a tradition similar to middle names among Humans. As with them, though, it's not a universal thing but I quite like it."

"I see. It's an interesting concept, especially for someone who presents as Hygran. Additional names are usually seen as vulgar, I suppose, and a little bit demeaning. As if people could forget your unique features and demand more."

"It's certainly one way to look on things."

The gunship lifted off and prepared to depart, swiftly followed by several more. The L-L bay doors opened and the convoy of gunships hurtled out, turning toward the damaged dreadnought.

"I'm checking out the *Ambari's* systems," Morix said, flinching after a few seconds. "Oh dear, what a mess."

"Tell me I didn't break the Imperial-era dreadnought," the Commodore said with a sigh.

The UIPE gave him a worried look.

"I can still insert myself into its network so we won't need the Golden Horizon repair facilities, but the ship is still fragile and will be until we can repair the system damage."

"Big guns are only good if we can fire them."

"Exactly."

From the outside the vessel appeared undamaged, but Alanar knew there was serious damage to the actual electronic systems that enabled the external components to function. How it occurred was due to a multitude of reasons all related to stringspace over-exposure.

On modern vessels the effects were irritating more than life threatening, as long as the jumps were not too numerous. But on vessels like the *Ambari*, even with protective measures, things could become very serious. In the Founder's War, the Rebellion had destroyed an entire fleet of dreadnoughts using a virus to initiate a twenty-five fast-jump sequence. The results had been mostly predictable until the fleet accidentally crashed into a rebel stronghold world, killing millions and wiping out a fleet stationed there. An impressive military irony.

The gunships made their final approach on the Hygran warship and began landing. Alanar's was first to land and as the doors slid open he was treated to the sight of a very stressed looking Ship-Commander Holon and two of his subordinates wearing similar expressions.

"Ship-Commander, I'm sorry about the damage," the Commodore apologised, climbing out. "I think we'll take the scenic route back to Hygra."

"I couldn't agree more, Commodore. If you wish to retain your flag aboard the *Watchman* I will not be surprised."

"Nonsense! We'll have you back up and running in no time. Hence why I brought some company." He smiled as the other gunships began landing around them. "Ten teams of Confederation Navy engineers, led by the *Vigilant Watchman*'s own Engineering Officer."

Holon's expression immediately became relieved.

"Thank you, Sir. I'll put my own chief engineer in touch with them."

He glanced at one of the subordinates at his side who broke away to approach one of the gunships which Maria was climbing out of. Morix29 gave a short cough.

"This is my UIPE second-in-command, Morix29. I believe you met at the briefing." Alanar introduced her with a gesture of the hand.

"Good to see you again, Ship-Commander. May I begin connections with your systems?" the tiny figure answered. "Much as I enjoy being so limited in size, I'd prefer to increase my capabilities."

"Of course, Morix29," Holon assented. "Though I am concerned with our ship in this condition that you will be equally limited."

The UIPE closed her eyes and flared away, reappearing seconds later in full size next to Alanar.

"Don't worry. You'd be surprised at how little processing capacity I need to function fully."

The Hygran Ship-Commander's eyes widened, marvelling at the technology before him. He nodded slowly.

"Shall we go to the bridge and get settled in?" he suggested.

"Yes, that would be wise," agreed Alanar. "While the ship is being repaired I have an idea of how to spend our time here."

They began walking towards the exit.

"I want to take the ship to the colony and meet with the Head of the Governing Council," Alanar continued. "Once all the survivors are rescued we won't be able to keep them aboard the Navy starships indefinitely. I thought that we might be able to put them up on the surface once they are processed."

"Obviously, as far apart from each other as we can get them," put in Morix. "The last thing anyone wants is a ground war on a vital colony."

"The Navy might have to subsidise the operation a great deal," Holon said. "The colony is still young by most standards. Due to its status it doesn't receive the level of support worlds in the Colonial Diet do and Hygra's resources are heavily committed elsewhere. High technology is limited to say the least."

He was right. It was easy to forget that in this day and age there were still worlds that did not have anti-grav, nano-tech and mass-scale fusion power. It was the reason the colony itself had not responded to the in-system battle. The colonial profile stated the planet's sensors were mostly trained inwards and even if it had reasonable coverage it could only have responded with five defence cutters.

"Swordships are outfitted with refugee assistance packages, but only for standard Humanoids. Specialist equipment will be required for the Winn Winn, but the Tardigs will be alright if we put them in a tropical area," added Morix.

"Yes, the Winn Winn will be difficult to say the least," Holon agreed. "I doubt Second Hygra's oceans will be suitable to sustain them. However, perhaps the Council or Governor will have an idea."

They arrived on the bridge, a protrusion on the topside of the aged military starship, several minutes later. Its layout was different from that aboard the swordship with a more cramped feel and dimmer lighting. All the consoles were lined up in rows split by a central aisle. All had a single large screen on them and all faced the huge screen before them that only showed a virtual reality 3-D display of the local space, littered with tactical icons. It would never change to any other type of display, a symbol of the rigidity of the old Imperial days.

"Obviously the seating and controls had to be modified for a purely Hygran crew, but for the most part the *Ambari* is exactly how it was when it was first launched," explained Holon. "Well...apart from the battle damage that had to be repaired."

"Battle damage?" asked Alanar.

"Before it was taken over by the Defence Directorate, the ship was stationed at the mothball yards over Centau Beta. Its last action before that was engaging two other ships at the Battle of Shokkar's Reach."

"One of the last battles of the war. Impressive," noted Morix. "Wait – two ships? Which side was it on?"

"Apparently, it was crewed entirely by telekinetic Centaurians and ran into two purely telepath Centaurian ships. There was a firefight and eventually it got boarded. By the time Human military support arrived one ship was destroyed, the others were in ruins and only about a dozen combatants survived."

They must have hated each other so badly at that point, Alanar thought.

History books could only bring so much of that back to life sometimes. There was no escaping its brutality, though. Shokkar's Reach had been a telekinetic enclave, one of the last not inside the war zones of the Empire. A quarter of a million civilians and tens of thousands of military personnel all completely wiped out in two weeks of close quarters fighting. A massacre, called a battle by those who usually failed to recognise the tragedy of the Founder's War.

"Well, the restoration team obviously did a fine job of it," Alanar complimented, looking intently at the tactical display.

It showed the fleet continuing to disperse across the system and the disabled vessels occasionally fuzzing out due to the fast-jump damage. This slow pace would probably continue for another hour or so until SLIDE capability returned. Until then they would only have sub-light systems to work with. Then an idea came to him.

"Can we contact the colony?" he asked an occupant of a communications console.

"At this range and given the damage to our systems, Commodore, real-time communication would be patchy at best."

"What about a comm-packet?"

"Only if we could locate a receiver and our sensors would take time to do so."

"With your agreement, Ship-Commander, I'd like to begin the effort to do so while we move on the colony?" Alanar asked.

"Completely, Commodore. My crew is at your disposal." Holon nodded at the operator. "I'll lay in the course myself. I assume this has something to do with the colony's defence fleet?"

"It does indeed. It might take us hours to get there but seconds for them."

The two Hygrans smirked at each other and Morix29 shook her head quietly.

"I'm going to assist the repair crews and see if we cannot move this along a little," she declared before flaring away.

Holon glanced at Alanar.

"I believe Humans would call her something of a free spirit."

"Depends on the Human. I imagine they'd have a few other phrases for her, too."

The tactical display changed to show a green line leading to Second Hygra, the dreadnought's course.

"Repairs will not be completed for another hour at least," Holon pointed out.

"Yes, I was thinking the same thing."

"And the handy thing about being in command is being able to control duty shifts. I have not eaten since we were advised to head to the base. Would you care to join me, Commodore?"

"As long as it's not going to impair the functions of the ship."

Holon motioned to the exit and the pair left, making their way toward the galley. As they did so Alanar used his synth-sym to view the operational history of the craft. It was unclear in several places given the fact it was a former rebel vessel and it'd had a pretty rough ride. Those sections that were legible were still fascinating, though.

It hadn't always been a rebel ship. It had been built over Centau Alpha shortly before the war broke out and had been assigned to patrol the mid-range colonies close to the core. In a daring assault in the first months of the war, a rebel strike force took the ship and used it in a series of raids and capture missions on the mid-range.

It later joined in a direct assault by the rebels on the Imperial capital that ultimately failed. After this its records became blurry for three years before re-emerging for certain after the rebels were pushed out of the core worlds and the Empire began constructing more ships.

In response it was sent to Talan'klee along with an armada of rebel ships to provide the 'muscle' for the rebel fleet and army assigned to defend the planet until it was taken by the Empire's Human shock-troops in the final years of the war. The *Ambari* was permanently engaged in battle until Shokkar's Reach when it appeared to be trying to evacuate with the remnants of the rebel fleet. If it hadn't been for the opposing warships it may well have linked up with its compatriots as they readied themselves to flee the galaxy or wherever it was that the telekinetics had vanished to. Colourful indeed.

They reached the galley area which, unlike the rest of the ship, was mostly devoid of activity.

"I believe the synthesisers were undamaged in the transit," Holon said, walking over to a console with a small portal next to it – one of several. "Once the key objectives have been achieved I'll have a proper meal made to celebrate if there is time."

"I think I'll have to institute it fleet-wide after what I put everyone through," Alanar replied, approaching another console.

Both typed in various codes and the closed portals opened moments later, revealing trays with various viscous pastes and pellets in their facets. They removed them and wandered over to a window-side table with a sadly unremarkable view of open space as Muthavia was behind them and Second Hygra ahead.

"I meant to ask how long you had served in the HDD, Ship-Commander?"

"Far, far too long, Commodore," the man said, laughing. "It'll be fifty-two years next month, actually."

"You should be running the place!"

"Oh, no! I like my command here enough. How about you and the Confederation Navy?"

"I'm ashamed to say only ten years – eleven in another seven months."

Holon whistled.

"And they gave you a command with…so many ships? You must have friends in high places."

Alanar narrowed his eyes.

"What were you going to say originally, Ship-Commander? And don't try and work your way around it."

"I meant nothing by it, Commodore. I –"

Alanar raised a finger and waved it from side to side. Holon sighed, obviously deciding to be honest.

"Ship-Commander Navat, there's something you should probably know about her," he began. "She's not easy to work with, especially with regards to Confederation or pro-Confederation elements."

Alanar smiled.

"Don't worry, Ship-Commander, I am well aware of Navat's problematic status and have dealt with it how I see fit," he reassured his subordinate.

"I see. In which case I apologise for implying you were incapable," apologised Holon.

"You had my best interests at heart. I just wish all my officers thought the same."

Holon's smile quickly returned at that. Alanar had to admit that despite the splendour of the *Vigilant Watchman*, the *Ambari* was more homely and welcoming, despite the damage and crampedness. They began eating and Alanar quickly discovered how hungry he was. It had been a while since he had eaten and if he was going to have to negotiate with a colonial government and two warring races, it would be a while before the chance came round again.

Despite not looking as appetising as the real food served on civilian vessels, or on special military occasions, the synthesised produce was certainly not lacking in taste and nutritional value. The Commodore could already feel his depleted strength being restored, by no means a bad thing given what lay ahead.

"Have you ever been to Second Hygra, Ship-Commander?" he asked after a few mouthfuls.

"Not recently, no. But I imagine it is as beautiful as my last visit. Yourself?"

"Never been. I doubt the pictures and holos do it service, frankly. Hopefully, we'll manage to get some surface time at some point."

Holon smiled broadly.

"I think every Hygran in the fleet would enjoy that, Commodore, as I imagine would the Population Oversight Board."

The pair laughed, somewhat downplaying the real importance of Second Hygra to the Hygran people as a whole. The planet was one of only two planets known to possess the conditions in which conception could occur. The government had tried cloning and in vitro-fertilisation treatments but the hard truth was that the Hygran genetic code – like that of most other species – was not amenable to cloning and their reproductive cycle too complicated for all but the most intense outside intervention.

The only option left was to conceive children as part of a stable family unit, though the abundance of wealth and access to health care in the Confederation essentially meant that this set-up was practical for all Hygrans. Should anything ever happen to the homeworld, at least there could be a back-up while the numbers recovered. More concrete was the concern that Hygrans made up such a small percentage of the general population of the Confederation. Second Hygra was essential in remedying that.

"I'll be sure to send them a report on the matter," assured Alanar. "I'm rather looking forward to meeting the Colony-Governor on that note, too."

"Ah, yes. Akshell. She certainly does have the whole package, doesn't she?"

The Colony-Governor was renowned for her intelligent, elegant management strategies and solutions, along with her great beauty. She was a Second Hygran born and bred, with two parents who also shared that distinction, ensuring her complete dedication to Second Hygra's advancement.

"Hmm," the Commodore agreed. "I hope she will be amenable to our request for support. My UIPE wasn't confident, though."

"Could go either way. On one hand she's dedicated to Second Hygra, including its security. On the other, Second Hygra is...well, it's not a core world by any definition."

Alanar nodded, thoughtfully. He considered the possibility of just going it alone with the Confederation Navy's resources. It was possible he supposed but steam-rolling the local colonist populace and government wasn't exactly the greatest way to go about things. No, the colony would be consulted. Any contribution would be welcomed.

"I suppose we'll find out soon enough. After all –"

"Captain and Commodore to command," came Morix's voice over the intercom. "Repeat! Captain and Commodore to command. Your presence is urgently required!"

"Looks like your free spirit is more efficient than we thought," speculated Holon.

"Or she's accidentally pissed off those defence cutters," Alanar only half-joked as they began making their way back to where they had come from.

Upon entering the bridge, Alanar first saw Morix29's holographic self projected to normal scale. She wore a rather mixed expression, something which concerned him greatly.

"Would you like the good news or the bad news first?"

At least her sense of humour was unchanged.

"Always good news first, please," replied Alanar.

"Very well. The good news is we have made contact with colonial representatives. The bad news is they are aboard three defence cutters refusing to let us any further into the system without speaking to you first."

The Commodore stopped short of swearing out loud and gauged the situation. It made sense in a way that the local defence force wouldn't know that the taskforce was due to arrive. Fleet movements were highly classified. Only high-ups would need to know. But what didn't make sense was the need for his presence. Morix29 had the appropriate authorisation to get them to co-operate.

"Why?"

"Something about wanting a Hygran to speak to about entry into sovereign ground."

Now he did swear.

"Put them through."

A screen next to her lit up with the face of a Hygran ship-commander. He looked incredibly stern for a young male.

"This is Confederation Commodore Alanar, Commander of the joint fleet on mission in your system. I understand we have an issue here. To whom am I speaking?"

"I am Squadron-Commander Leshtek. My apologies, Commodore. I wished merely to speak with the commander of this force before letting it pass into my jurisdiction."

Maybe he looked so stern because he held such a demanding position for his age. Nevertheless...

"And my second-in-command didn't quite cut it because..."

"Not to be rude, Commodore, but I prefer to talk with beings with real authority in these kinds of situations, especially...unconstructed ones."

That caught him off guard. Morix rolled her eyes at the comment. Clearly she had already had this conversation.

"Well, you have spoken to me now, Squadron-Commander, and I am forwarding you our credentials – again. I assume it will be good enough this time?"

Leshtek nodded.

"Of course, Commodore. My ships stand ready to assist."

"Very good. In that case, may I request use of one of your cutters to take myself and some staff to the colonial capital?"

"Naturally. I'll personally escort you in my command craft."

"Excellent. You may expect us shortly. Alanar out."

Leshtek nodded once and disappeared.

Morix, Ship-Commander. Walk with me."

The trio stalked through the corridors of the dreadnought moments later, heading to no destination in particular.

"Prep my gunship, Morix. I'd also like you to accompany me and the Ship-Commander, if you are both willing," he began, noting their nods as he continued. "Now, while we wait, would someone care to tell me what the fuck that was all about? Why do I have the guns of Hygran defence cutters pointing at my ships with the belligerence of a Na'thax swarm?"

"I'd put it down to the stress of his position and young age," offered Holon. "Especially given the recent events."

"I concur," agreed Morix. "Though I could have done without the complication, he's obviously stressed and looking for an outlet."

"By picking a fight with a dreadnought?" Alanar shook his head.

"More insane things have happened." Morix shrugged. "I'll dedicate a partition to do some digging if it will set you at ease."

He blew out his cheeks.

"No, we don't have time. Let's meet the colonials and get a plan to deal with these casualties drawn up," he decided. "Launching an investigation into Defence Directorate personnel isn't part of our remit."

That drew a narrowing of the eyes from Morix but she said nothing. They made their way to the gunships, making arrangements as they went. Holon placed his second-in-official-command of the ship and Alanar called Officer Anderson via synth-sym.

"Yes, Commodore?"

"I'm sorry to bother you, Officer, but we contacted the colony much sooner than I thought we might."

"Ah right, those defence cutters. I heard."

"Yes, I am taking a small group to the colony to meet with the government via one of the cutters. I want to discuss plans for setting up holding sites for the battle casualties! Can you spare some staff to consult with?"

She paused momentarily, probably checking over the situation around her.

"I have a capable staff here, Commodore. I can join you with one of my subordinates."

"That's great, Officer. You're sure?"

"Yes, Sir. I think my presence here is only serving to irritate the Hygran chief down here. However, I would like to take one of the *Ambari* crew with us to advise on Hygran technical specs."

"I'll run the request by Ship-Commander Holon."

He paused to compose a message to his subordinate with his mind. The positive response was near instantaneous.

"Pick your people and we'll see you on the deck, Officer."

"Very good, Commodore."

The link ended and the march towards the gunships continued. When they arrived, the Officer and her pair of cohorts were waiting for them by one of the wasp-like support craft.

"I have to say, Officer Anderson, your promptness is very refreshing," Alanar complimented, smiling.

"Thank you, Sir."

They climbed into the cabin and the vessel lifted off, closing its doors as it did so, before shooting into space to round on the Hygran defence cutters. The trio held a standard arrowhead offensive formation before the stalled dreadnought, with the Squadron-Commander's vessel as the lead ship.

What do they think they are playing at, Alanar wondered, staring at the formation.

In the Founder's War only three space navies had faced off against the marauding Centaurian titans (arguably only two if the 21st Century Human shuttles and high atmo-suborbital fighters were discounted). Two wielded craft larger than the cutters with equal firepower and all three had been wiped out in seconds. Still, he supposed it was all about appearances in the end.

The gunship skipped straight toward the lead cutter as the vessel opened a small bay entrance on its topside, revealing two small shuttles and barely enough space for the Confederation craft.

"How...quaint," Morix muttered.

They landed softly and slid back the doors after re-pressurisation. Leshtek was walking to them briskly as a brief vibration rolled through the cutter.

"We entered stringspace the moment you came aboard, Commodore," he said, saluting. "Welcome aboard the *Raltar*."

You've changed your tune, Alanar thought, returning the salute.

"Interesting name," he said instead.

"Yes, after the resistance hero in the war."

The Commodore gave a small smile, suppressing an eyeroll. Of course.

"Commodore," called Morix from the gunship, "may I transfer myself to your network?"

He nodded and continued to walk towards the Squadron-Commander.

"May I ask the estimated time of arrival?"

"Less than a minute. But the crew mess has been cleared so we can view the Orbital Transport Ring when we emerge."

"Thank you, Squadron-Commander. I'd like to use your communication system to contact the government afterwards."

Leshtek smiled.

"Already done, Commodore. Arrangements are already being made. Now, please come this way."

Alanar raised his eyebrows in surprise as he was led to the mess hall cum observation deck. This was not the reception he had been expecting.

The group emerged from corridors into a room with a view of space blossoming as the cutter re-entered normal space over Second Hygra. The planet was beautiful and could easily have been mistaken for the original upon first glance. It bore a clear atmosphere around its equatorial regions on the dayside, showing lush forests, high mountain ranges and a gigantic set of coral reefs.

The most immediate difference between this world and the homeworld was the lack of sprawling mega-cities, which were visible on Hygra whether it was day or night. The sole huge settlement on the planet must have been on the nightside. This left only one sign on Second Hygra as evidence of its habitation: a gigantic silvery band running at a forty-five degree angle all around it. An Orbital Transport Ring.

Utilising magnetic levitation, super strength and flexible materials, an OTR enabled the movement of any material into space or onto any location around a planet at minimal cost in all aspects.

Originally built as part of an elevator system to ship goods to and from the colony, it had been expanded to enable quick transport around the globe and as part of greater plans to turn the colony into a major trading outpost. As more and more emigrants and ships arrived, it would be utilised to seed more mega-cities and support systems, transforming the planet into an exact replica of the homeworld.

"Beautiful," breathed Maria Anderson in awe.

Everyone smiled or nodded in agreement as the sun glinted off the thin ribbon of metal ringing the globe. As it did so a freighter came into view as it came around the planet from the capital, followed by two smaller vessels. Pleasure-cruisers.

The ship lingered for a moment longer before moving in closer to the planet, slowly but surely. The group remained silent as the view changed from the daylight side with its spectacular vistas to the terminator and nightside.

Initially little was visible, not ever the TR, but this quickly changed when the capital city came into sight.

Due to the effort Hygrans had to put into creating families and rearing young, not to mention the long gestation periods and massive resource investments, it only made sense they pulled together socially, politically and economically. Hence the creation of the mega-cities was rooted deep in the psyche of the Hygran people. Indeed, even on modern Hygra there were only two dozen on the surface. Despite this, the urban concentrations took up massive swathes of land, even conquering mountains and seas in the process. The similar methodology behind their creation made them vast but nowhere near identical.

So, when Alanar laid eyes on the city he saw something new, but also had a feeling of déjà vu. It sprawled for at least a hundred kilometres in every direction, fragmenting only slightly when it came to the ocean. All of it was lit up from the edge of the piers and extraction facilities to its beating heart of gigantic skyscrapers reaching miles into the sky to touch the edge of space. The tallest didn't even stop there, stretching up to the OTR to connect it to the surface.

"We have received a communiqué from the colony," Leshtek said quietly, obviously using inserts or some variation thereof. "The Colony-Governor will receive you on the roof of Government Tower to begin discussions."

"Excellent," Alanar replied.

The group marched out back to the gunship and loaded back into the cabin. The Squadron-Commander waved at them one last time before leaving to allow the room to re-pressurise, enabling them to depart.

As the vessel hurtled towards the surface it fell past the ring into the atmosphere, aiming for a clear space well outside of the mega-city. Despite the urgency of the mission, safety was paramount. The damage that could be inflicted by a boat travelling at such massive speeds, crashing into the base of a space elevator, was potentially catastrophic.

Within ten minutes it had smashed through the atmosphere and occupied the airspace two kilometres above the world, its surface currently a man-grave jungle according to external sensors. The pilots turned toward the city, illuminating the horizon like a burning sun. It was even possible to see the connection towers from this distance.

"We'll be at the capital in five minutes," reported one of the pilots. "The Governor is awaiting us."

They carried on over the surface, dropping lower and lower and gaining speed. At first only small streets and farms scattered the ground below, then there were more lights, more buildings, higher, larger structures as they progressed further and further. Eventually, the towers that made up the bulk of the city were more clearly defined, including the great spire of Government Tower, where the Colony-Governor and Colony-Councillors lived and worked.

"Not very well resourced, eh?" Alanar chuckled to Morix.

"It's deceptively original Hygran-looking, isn't it?" the UIPE partially conceded. "But bear in mind that OTRs are fairly basic technology combinations, as are star-scrapers. And, of course, the whole thing is run on either solar, wind or tidal power. It's all done for minimal cost and maximum output and expansion. All imported, naturally."

"Really?"

"Hmm. Give it another century or two and it'll be a more accurate replica of the homeworld it seeks to emulate. At least, technology-wise."

The gunship rose slightly and banked towards Government Tower, flying to its roof, shooting over it, then coming down on a platform jutting out from its edge. Waiting at the edge, wearing a very formal-looking white and red outfit, and joined by a dozen other formally-dressed officials, was a female Hygran of outstanding beauty and height. Colony-Governor Akshell. Alanar made a bee-line for her as he marched off the gunship.

"Commodore Alanar," she greeted him with a smile and extended her hand. "It is good to meet you finally. Welcome to Second Hygra. I gather the trip here didn't go well for your entire fleet?"

"A pleasure to meet you, too, Colony-Governor," he replied with a smile and shook her hand. "My ships will be fine, just some minor fast-jump damage. This is Ship-Commander Holon of the *Ambari*, Engineering Officer Maria Anderson of the *Vigilant Watchman* and their advisory team. I have also got the UIPE Morix29 inside my neural interface to assist."

Akshell nodded at all of them bar Morix, her smile broadening.

"You are all very welcome. Though I am curious, Commodore, how my colony can help you with your current mission?"

"I'd like to have places to house the battle casualties when the Navy ships retrieve them, just while we negotiate, and wondered if we might use part of the colony and any materials you might be able to spare."

She frowned slightly as she thought.

"We'll certainly do our best. Come with me and I'll introduce you to my government. We'll see if we can get you your rescue space."

They were briefly introduced to the rest of the council before being ushered down to the meeting room where the Colony-Governor held most of her important discussions. Once they were seated, Alanar started his proposal, with Morix29 on the screen behind him for support.

"First of all, I'd like to apologise for disrupting your plans at this late hour, but it won't be long before the Navy vessels begin retrieving the first battle casualties," he began. "There is not going to be enough room to treat all of them with maximum efficiency, or house them afterwards. Therefore, I would like to request designated areas to house both sets of combatants while I negotiate with the Tardig government and the Winn Winn crews."

"That seems perfectly reasonable, Commodore," said one of the councillors, his colleagues nodding in agreement. "But I also heard something about resources."

"Yes. Well, the Winn Winn aren't the easiest people to cater for being quasi-amphibious cephalopods, unable to stay in open air long. While the Navy ships are equipped to relocate the Tardigs, they cannot support many Winn Winn in this situation. So, we wondered if the colony could help in that regard."

"How?"

Alanar glanced at Morix who took over.

"I've analysed your colonial inventory for ways of supporting the Winn Winn and have identified several facilities that could be used," she explained, shrinking her image in the screen to accommodate several maps, designs and images. "University buildings, scientific research areas, two aquariums and even an undersea mining structure, could all be utilised for the effort. Full agreement and compliance are essential, though, not to mention the acceptance of the impact this will have on the colony economy."

"I see," said Akshell. "And how many of these places do you need access to?"

"Ideally, all of them. But we are aware of the colony's needs," replied Alanar. "Essentially, we'll take whatever we can get."

She looked at a councillor.

"Yothol, how long would it take to reconfigure the largest of the Koroposol holding areas?"

"Well, I'm no expert on the scientific areas or aquarium management," the woman confessed. "But that mining structure and the university sites in the north and east could be re-tooled in, say, six hours."

"Excellent!" Akshell turned back to Alanar. "Good enough?"

He smiled. "Perfect."

One Councillor coughed to interrupt. The same male as before.

"That uni-site in the north is currently being used for a community project by my district. I'd prefer not to have to cancel it."

"I'm sorry, Councillor, but I've made my decision. When this is over I'll fully compensate you for the loss," said Akshell.

"If it's any consolation I, too, will ask the Confederation Navy to help with undoing the effects of our mission here," assured the Commodore.

The Councillor nodded but said nothing. A cracked egg in the making of an omelette. Alanar could only look very apologetic before carrying on.

"Now, with regard to the Tardigs. We could drop them off in the tropics under guard but I'd prefer equal treatment. With that in mind, I would like an area to set up our assistance centres. Perhaps a park dome or something?"

"New Century and Landing are our biggest," Yothol suggested. "They are also quite close, relatively speaking, and warm enough that they will be comfortable."

Another Councillor, this one female, shook her head.

"Landing Park is too close to the eastern uni-site. I don't want a war breaking out on my home turf if they start fighting."

"The Navy ships have several thousand marines on board for security and your own personnel would be welcome to participate, too," Alanar assured her. "Security is our priority after helping out, naturally."

"Very good, Commodore," the councillor said acidly. "Because I've seen what these people do to each other first-hand and it's not pretty!"

"Indeed," he agreed. "If there are no more concerns we can get into the more intricate details of this operation."

Looks were exchanged. No-one else seemed to be disturbed by what was about to take place.

"Very well," Akshell said quietly and briskly. "Let's get to work, people. It's going to be a hectic day.

                *   *   *

Several hours later, Alanar stood on the roof of Government Tower, taking a break from the co-ordination efforts downstairs. The first stages of alterations were well underway now with Maria and her advisor consulting at the three Winn Winn sites and Morix and Holon remaining with him. Everything seemed to be going smoothly, both on the colony and in space.

All the Hygran craft, including the *Ambari*, were now either patrolling around the system or hanging in orbit making final preparations to do so. The Navy craft were about to make their first excursions to the damaged vessels, expecting to make the initial drop-off within the next two hours. By then, with any luck, the colony would almost be ready to receive its guests.

He was slightly worried, though. The Tardig government was yet to get in touch about its ships. That made him wonder. Surely at least a scout would have been despatched to investigate. So far, though, nothing had been heard around the perimeter. That being said, the Republic wasn't exactly known for caring about the needs of its military crews too much. It had access to vast armadas of ships and hundreds of millions of active troops – a military massively superior in numbers to the Confederation's despite it occupying less territory. This probably meant an even bigger bureaucracy.

The Commodore sighed heavily. Sometimes the Galaxy could be so uncaring. He supposed that was why the Republic had invested so much in its military.

"Well, great minds evidently do think alike."

He started and turned to see Akshell standing behind him with a small white cylinder in her mouth that had one end lit.

"I often come out here to relax," she explained before frowning. "Sorry if I startled you."

"Not a problem, Colony-Governor –"

"Akshell, please."

He nodded.

"Akshell," he repeated, staring at the cylinder. "I wasn't aware that you smoked."

"Only if I'm drinking privately or when my work keeps me up late," she confessed. "Though I'd still prefer it if the free press didn't find out."

"I understand. Your secret is safe with me."

"I can put it out if it bothers you."

"Not at all. May I ask how you started? It's something of a rarity these days."

"Trip to Earth when I was younger. One of my roommates introduced me to it. Would you believe he's the Earth Ambassador to Hygra now?!"

They smiled at each other.

"I don't think there's a more unusual race in the Confederation," she continued. "So much difference. So many cultures. So many ways to poison yourself!"

"Hmm, true. Personally I prefer a bit more stability. Probably why I usually get on best with the Humans in the Navy."

An OTR elevator, a massive cubical object attached to one of the connection towers, shot up into space in front of them. They watched in silence for a few moments until it disappeared from view.

"We based it on the one at Earth," Akshell said quietly. "A few things were copied from it, actually. Not exact, given what we had to work with, but it does the job."

"So, you're a Humano-phile then?"

She laughed.

"Not quite. We've also incorporated things from Hygra, Talan'klee and Centau Alpha. I suppose you could say I'm more of a homeworld lover, really. My predecessors had more of a penchant for Hygra. I felt it was detrimental."

"How so?"

"Our future is not solely tied to the homeworld, Commodore. Second Hygra is linked to the rest of the Confederation, too. I think it is best that Second Hygra represents a link to our past *and* future."

"A fine sentiment."

"Thank you. I wish some of my councillors agreed."

"I hold the same views about some of my officers."

She smirked.

"Not easy, is it?"

"Not really, no. Nothing worthwhile ever is, though."

"My father said the same thing."

A live uplink alert from his synth-sym told him Lal-ne-vo was requesting an audience.

"Excuse me, but I must take a call," he said.

"By all means."

He accepted the call and Lal-ne-vo's face appeared on the virtual plane.

"Captain! How goes the retrieval?"

"Very well, thank you. We have established forward processing points on all vessels and are moving further aboard. But there is an issue you are required to assist with."

"Really? Such as?"

"We have contacted one of the command staff of a Winn Winn vessel, but she is refusing to relinquish her position or indeed her weapon without speaking to the commanding officer for the mission."

"What?!" He almost laughed incredulously. Did the officer seriously think she could hold out against a Navy force?

"She wants to speak to the highest Confederation authority in the system immediately about a matter of the greatest urgency. This would be fine if she wasn't injured and her formsuit wasn't failing."

Alanar threw his hands up and sighed heavily, knowing where this was going.

"Indeed. I apologise, Commodore, but I would much appreciate your assistance in this matter."

"Alright. I'll call one of the defence cutters and hitch a ride out. Keep her calm until I get there."

"I've already made arrangements."

The link was terminated and he turned to look at the Colony-Governor, sending a request to the Squad-Commander at the same time.

"It never stops, does it?" she said knowingly, before flicking her cigarette away. "Trouble?"

"Apparently a Winn Winn officer is raising hell over something that I need to deal with personally."

"I see. You are popular, indeed."

A reply came back from Leshtek. They were dispatching a shuttle for a fly-by pick up. Wonderful.

"Well, it's supposed to happen when you take command, so I'm told."

"Only in the military, Commodore. In politics it's not so simple."

"I'm sure you'd do as well in this profession as you do in your own."

Her face fell a little at that.

"I used to think so, Commodore. And for a time I even considered the HDD. But when I saw and heard of what goes on across the border I quickly reconsidered that option," she confessed.

"The Confederation is different from the Republic, though," argued Alanar. "We haven't fought a war in centuries. Battles aren't even battles anymore."

"Yes, but how long can we keep it like that? You forget that this isn't just the border with the Tardigs, it's close to the border with the Open Galaxy, too. We hear things from traders, travellers and the occasional non-Winn Winn refugees that pass through."

The Commodore tilted his head a little.

"And...?"

"There are rumours – and that's all I'm saying they are – that the Republican military is attacking isolated worlds, colonies, sometimes entire systems. Maybe two or three dozen. Most of the time it's justified as attempts to stabilise the areas around their civilisation, but there's no denying the aggressive nature of the operations."

"The Open Galaxy is a pretty wild area, Akshell. And the Tardig's foreign policy, excluding when it comes to the Confederation, of course, reflects that accordingly. I think you might be hearing the voices of the disaffected on that matter –"

"I have considered that, but you must understand that this is my home. I need every possible piece of information to ensure its safety. That's why I'm rather glad the Navy is here. I'm worried not about the Republic, Commodore. I'm worried about who or what they might drive here in their crusade for stability."

The sound of a shuttle approaching thrummed in the distance.

"I see. Look, once this mission is over I'll make a recommendation to the Navy to place a more long-term force here to support you. In exchange for shore leave privileges, of course."

The pair smiled at each other again.

"As long as you get to lead that mission, too. I'll do my best. My people and I work best with familiar faces."

The small Hygran craft was nearer now and visible. Time to go soon.

"It's a beautiful world, Akshell. I wouldn't leave unless it was totally necessary."

"Well, we do try our best. Good luck with your Winn Winn officer. We'll try to have everything ready by the time you return."

The shuttle was overhead now, dangling a wire with a foothold attached close to the ground. Alanar placed his foot in it and was hoisted up.

"Thank you, Akshell," he called back, "and call me Alanar."

She waved as he ascended into the belly of the craft and the doors closed underneath him. There to greet him was the Squad-Commander.

"Welcome aboard, Commodore," he said. "We'll have you in situ in about five minutes."

"Do you always take such an active role in the running of your squadron?"

They sat opposite each other in a row of seats in the cabin.

"Always. I'm present on every mission of importance and change my command craft regularly."

"Not a bad idea. Thank you for the assistance."

"That's alright. The sooner we can get you there, the sooner things get done."

The shuttle breached the atmosphere and slid past the OTR's silvery structure, heading for the orbiting defence cutter. As they prepared to dock, Alanar considered what Akshell had told him. Though he had tried to reassure her, he couldn't help but feel a little disturbed by the news of the Tardig operations. The Confederation should have heard something about it, at the very least from the Republic itself.

The two powers made up the largest military forces in the galaxy and the Tardigs themselves visited the Confederation and vice-versa, always being careful and polite. Surely they must have known about what was happening? He made a mental note to interview one of the Tardigs about it. If it were true, Command might like a report about it.

He put his head on the headrest, relaxed and closed his eyes. The Colony-Governor was right about the burdens of command.

"Shall we stay with the Navy vessels while you are aboard?" asked Leshtek.

"It's alright. I'll return to the colony with the casualties and set up the defence perimeter. Actually, I'd like your help with that. You know the local space much better than I do," replied the Commodore, opening his eyes. "We can discuss it when I get back."

"Thank you, Commodore. It'll be good to do some actual military work for a change."

"Oh, by the way, Squadron-Commander, you don't happen to know anything about any unusual operations in Republic space, would you?"

Leshtek smiled and chuckled.

"The Colony-Governor and I have been friends since I was assigned here, Commodore, but I'll admit I think interstellar military strategy isn't her area of expertise."

"You think the rumours are false?"

The Squad-Commander nodded.

"We are positioned close to one of the Galaxy's most contested areas of space. The Winn Winn will do or say anything to hurt the occupation forces, including flying ships into cities. I don't think they'd have much of a problem spreading lies about our allies launching aggressive assaults on defenceless worlds."

"I see. That does make sense in a way."

"The HDD and Navy Security and Intelligence think the same thing, Sir. Akshell has had them both out here and they concluded the same thing: that the insurgents are behind the whole thing. It will only succeed in doing the exact opposite of what it is designed to do."

"Which is?"

"They want the rest of the Galaxy to hate the Tardigs as much as they do. For us to come riding to their rescue. It's not going to happen."

Alanar smiled.

"No, it's really not," he agreed. "They pretty much lost all support when they crashed that asteroid into one of their own moons!"

"Hmm... last thing I heard, the Biridians and the ISA were putting together assistance task forces to help the Republic."

"It's true. Just before I left they claimed they would be entering the field next year."

Leshtek began to reply but stopped short and paused for a few moments, clearly reviewing a message.

"We have arrived at our destination. The shuttle is launching for the damaged craft," he said finally.

The tiny craft lifted out of the hangar into the open space of the former battle zone. The area was littered with debris and the occasional remnants of the crews. On one side of the field were Winn Winn war-spheres, three desolated spherical vessels. On the other were the crumpled remnants of the Tardig attack frigate, a horn-profiled ship, and the elongated hammer form of a strike-cruiser. In between and amongst the two sides were the recognisable Confederation Navy ships and strings of support craft moving in between them and their assigned hulks. It was an awe-inspiring sight to behold.

The Hygran shuttle flitted over to one of the Winn Winn vessels, literally half destroyed by the battle, and landed inside on a support pad the rescue teams had set up. As soon as it landed, a set of stairs slid out and a side door opened. Alanar walked down them to greet Lal-ne-vo, briefly turning to wave to Leshtek, then moved further into the wreck.

"Situation?" he asked.

"She's not well, I'm afraid, Commodore. The formsuit is at critical. Shots have already been fired."

"I hope this works."

They reached the Marine perimeter a few moments later to be greeted by –

"I'll kill anyone who steps through that door! So help me, in the name of the homeland I'll riddle you all with holes!" a strained, high-pitched, accented squeal declared.

"That would be most unfortunate," Alanar replied firmly, "since I have come here specifically to see you."

"Who are you?" demanded the voice.

"Commodore Alanar, Commander of the Confederation Navy-Hygran Defence Directorate taskforce in this system. Who are you?"

There was a pause, punctuated by a suffocating choking noise.

"I am Controller Hyk'to'kel'na'scro'Gabari, Commander of the war-sphere *Chi'tok'shol'ree'Kabor*. I must speak with you and you alone, Commandore. No staff present."

"Your formsuit is badly damaged and you are armed. If I assist you with medi-gel, what is to stop you taking me hostage?"

That choking sound came again, followed by several hisses like gas escaping.

"Leave your medi-gel devices. I do not plan on needing them," the Winn Winn officer replied. "As for my weapon...I suppose a little trust is required on that part."

The Commodore thought for a moment, then turned to Lal-ne-vo.

"Dismissed, Captain," he ordered quietly.

"Yes, Commodore," it said before yelling to the Marines, "Marines, withdraw to the alpha-site."

"I'll see you there." Alanar nodded as the marines sauntered past. Then, shouting to the Controller, "My forces have withdrawn. I'm coming in."

He began to walk slowly around the corner into the ruined compartment of the vessel. It appeared to be – or had been – what would have passed for a communal area in the ship. It was littered with the dark, barely-recognisable forms of slaughtered Winn Winn, their bodies covered by the formsuits they all had to wear out of their naturally aquatic environment.

Usually the Winn Winn starships were filled with a water-like fluid designed to support them. In the current ruined state of their once advanced and vast empire, though, they were forced to utilise cheaper, more readily-available tactics and technology to support their resistance to the Tardigs. So, formsuits and fluid-less environments became the norm, much to the detriment of their race's performance and survival in space.

This was also why the figure he saw slouched against the far wall was more suit than actual Winn Winn, but for the huge holes that had been blasted in it, along with the occasional crack. It wrapped round the skin of the being inside, allowing it to use its manipulator tentacles normally and to stand upright, keeping its bulbous 'head' up in the air.

With the damage it had taken, the Winn Winn could barely clutch the bulky and primitive projectile weapon in its tendrils. And then there were those large, haunting eyes, already showing signs of glazing over permanently.

"They murdered everyone with an overload shot," it wheezed. "I tried to stop them, but they punched a hole clean through my power-pack."

He went over to her.

"I can still get you help," the Hygran said, placing a hand on the artificial carapace. "Please."

"No, this cannot wait. Datavise me your authorisation code. I...I don't have long."

Using his synth-sym, he did so.

"Ah, a recent promotion," the officer coughed. "I'm sorry such information must touch the young first."

A file was broadcast into Alanar's mind.

"Take this to your superiors, Commodore," the dying being hissed. "You must assist us. You must! Don't trust anyone under you!"

"What is it?" he demanded calmly.

"The proof...proof." She cough-wheezed.

"Proof? Proof of what?"

"That the enemy – the enemy is coming."

Luminous green fluid was seeping through the cracks. The Winn Winn was losing control over its internal regulation organs. The flow was rapidly increasing.

"What enemy? The Tardigs?"

"Yes, the enemy."

"Coming? Coming for who? You're not making any sense."

"Coming for EVERYONE!" she screamed before torrents of fluid flooded out of her and she died, drenching him in the process.

Alanar swore, throwing himself away from the corpse.

It was too late, of course. He was covered from head to toe. Waiting to analyse his data-packet until later, he stood, brushing off as much of the foul liquid as he could, and called Lal-ne-vo.

"Commodore, are you alright?"

"The Controller is dead, I'm afraid, and I'm not in a great state. Call a gunship to take me to the *Vigilant*. I want to speak to the Winn Winn you processed."

"Yes, Commodore. I have one standing by. Did she manage to tell you what she wanted?"

He remembered the Winn Winn's words.

"It was just gibberish. A commander distraught by the loss of her crew. I feel I should let the survivors know. I don't think there's much else I can do before we return to Second Hygra."

"I'm sure it will be appreciated. They are being held in the main mess area."

"I'll be with you shortly."

The link ended and he regarded the body of the former Controller. What had she been trying to warn him about? She cut such a sad figure, an allegory of what the insurgency was slowly becoming. He sighed and began walking towards the alpha-site.

When he arrived, Lal-ne-vo was clearly unnerved by his appearance. Alanar realised that part of Talan biology was probably responsible for that: to their sensitive noses he had the reek of death.

"Perhaps a shower and change of clothes would be advisable beforehand?" the Talan suggested as they boarded.

"I agree, Captain."

"There are Humanoid hygiene facilities on the *Vigilant*, but they are communal in nature, I'm afraid."

The Hygran gave a wry smile from his fluid-encrusted face, remembering his days as a Cadet and Crewman, and sometimes even as an Officer.

"Don't worry, Captain. I did my first few years of service at Star Haven. It doesn't get more communal than that."

He thought he caught a slight twitch in the Talan's antennae.

The gunship flitted over to the swordship, bypassing a queue of its kin and landing on the deck minutes later. The flight deck was a great deal less chaotic than the Commodore expected with casualties being placed on it in rows by marines and inspected and treated, or collected, by the medical crewmen assigned to the duty. It all looked very orderly but for the poor condition of most of the Winn Winn.

The vile fluid encrusted much of the floor from where the cephalopods had lost internal pressure regulation and slathered the deck. On his way to the washrooms, displayed in his head by the local AI, Alanar caught sight of the ship's Chief Medical Officer, a Centaurian covered in fluid much like that covering him. The Officer stood away from the Winn Winn she was treating, looked intently at the Hygran Crewman next to her and turned towards the Commodore.

Centaurians were one of the key founding races of both the Confederation and the Empire which preceded it. Standing over seven feet tall with slightly-scaled skin of massively varying shades of blue and purple (the Officer happened to be light blue) and large wide eyes set far apart. Their bodies were slender but strong, broad shoulders supporting a large pair of wings covered by feathers the same colour as those that crested their heads.

In spite of these vast external differences, it was their telepathy that really set them apart, enabling them to issue orders and pick them up very easily. It had also enabled them centuries ago to build a vast civilisation that had conquered a quarter of the Galaxy, enslaved several races and fought a brutal civil war. Unnerving was an understatement to describe the experience of those who were not used to them.

>Greetings, Commodore<, came the voice in his head as the Officer stood to attention. It was warm, feminine, yet somehow filled with strength. >May I help you?<

"Yes, I'd like to know a few things about the Winn Winn," began Alanar. "Have you treated any senior officers?"

>Only two. The rest were either killed in battle or died in the transfer over to the ship.<

"Ranks, please."

>I was unable to tell for certain given the damage, but they appeared to be ranked higher than Controllers. <

"I see. And how are they?"

A troubled expression rippled across the usually calm visage.

>Truthfully, Commodore, I have done my best, but I expect one of them to die in the next twenty-four hours and the other is traumatised to near catatonia. If you are going to debrief them, I highly recommend you do it soon.<

"Thank you, Officer. I'll let you get back to your work." Alanar said, smiling through the filth on his face.

The Centaurian nodded and turned, leaving him to stroll off the deck and towards the shower and wash facilities. On the way he earned a few stray odd glances at his appearance, but more of determination and respect. He imagined they probably thought he was voluntarily throwing himself into the effort and he liked to think he would if there wasn't so much else going on in the system.

Eventually, he reached the desired section of the ship. The Navy tried to cater as much as possible to the needs of its personnel, but sometimes it had to generalise. Humanoids had standardised wash facilities, as did avians, insectoids and the other life form types that crewed the warships. So, it wasn't surprising to see Humans, Hygrans and Kin-Sai, to name but a few species, altogether in these places.

He came to the locker room and found a free space. Datavising his access code and setting the locker to wash the clothes, he began stripping off. While he showered, the locker would flood with cleaner nanobots and make his uniform as good as new.

Turning from closing the full locker, he walked into the wash area where several showers were already heard running and fine steam filled the air. As he walked into the main room, a Human returning from it spotted him and snapped to attention.

"Commodore, on the deck!" he half-yelled, half-yelped and several other figures could be seen in the steam standing to attention.

Alanar stopped, slightly taken aback before allowing a humoured expression to fall across his face, exchanging a casual salute with the Human male.

"At ease all of you!" the Hygran replied, trying not to laugh. "At least until we have some clothes on!"

The rigid figures stood at ease and continued about their business, somewhat sheepishly. Alanar looked at the Human male, quickly identifying him via synth-sym as Marine Crewman Soro Shamel Not just any Human male, but an Earther no less.

"Crewman Shamel, while I admire your enthusiasm and professionalism, note that next time we're in this situation I'd prefer it if you would ignore protocol."

Shamel smiled and sharply nodded, clearly slightly embarrassed as he returned to his locker.

Alanar walked towards his chosen shower and began datavising further commands.

As the enhanced water washed over his filthy skin, he accessed the information uploaded to him by the Winn Winn Controller, shutting off access to the external network as he did so. He didn't want anyone else trying to look in on the review.

Opening the file he saw it was a series of media types with attached descriptions, schematics and an overview. Alanar moved through the thumbnail covers, viewing the extensive catalogue: One hundred and twelve images, a holographic-motion convertible and one hundred and fifty-four text files.

He selected an image file and it expanded in his mind's eye. It showed a massive Tardig formation of military vessels of all kinds, hanging in space over a seemingly heavily-populated world judging from the lights visible on the nightside. The planet looked oddly familiar so he opened the adjoining test which read:

Image Description and Analysis: - Tardig Republic Republican Guard 10th Assault Fleet over Chamena – three thousand ships on operations and preparatory battle manoeuvres.

There then followed a string of numbers detailing dates and co-ordinates and a list of ship types and counts. It couldn't be the case, though. Chamena was a small Winn Winn colony of that had been pacified relatively easily and quickly in the Tardig invasion. There was no need for an assault fleet to be stationed there, even if its population had expanded so quickly.

Another image showed an aerial view of a huge facility taken from high altitude. It seemed to consist of several hundred cuboid buildings of standardised size, surrounded by a perimeter wall with extensive defences.

Image Description and Analysis: - Tardig Republic Internal Security Concentrated Containment Facility 10251 E7. Location: Bloresh'ka. Population: 250,000+.

Bloresh'ka was an unpopulated rock, though. An ancient victim of the Hak'na'krena.

The next image was downright disturbing. It purported to show the 16th Assault Fleet attacking a planet labelled Lia'ket'abrin. Almost the entire globe was being ravaged by a firestorm raining down from the thousands of ships in orbit. Apparently this had taken place just over a week ago on Winn Winn mid-range space.

In the real world Alanar frowned hard. He selected the overview but it demanded an access code he didn't have. It appeared to be top level clearance. So he tried the holo instead. Same result. It appeared even he couldn't be trusted with the whole story. Maybe an interview with the two Winn Winn might give him some results.

He closed the file and reconnected himself to the network, rubbing off the last of the filth and deactivating the shower. What the hell was going on here? Assault fleets wandering the Galaxy, new settlements, burning worlds and classified files. Something was up.

Alanar reached the locker and began putting his clothes back on, now freshly washed by the cleaner systems. Once done he fired off a request to the *Watchman*'s AI to show him where the Winn Winn senior officers were being held. It answered near instantaneously: they were in a converted mess hall a few decks up.

The AI also provided a route to the area for which Alanar gave thanks. All Navy vessels were designed to have self-sufficient segments in the event the C3C was compromised, or the ship was boarded. As a result, bar any superficial decoration by the crew, the interiors could look depressingly similar to those who were new aboard.

As he made his way towards the mess hall the number of Marines, medics and casualties escalated rapidly. More and more were brought in all the time. It seemed as though the operation was accelerating. Maybe the casualties would be at Second Hygra sooner than they thought. Morix and the others had better be making good progress.

The mess hall was eerily quiet compared to the noise outside. Casualties were either laid sprawled on cots or suspended in fluid tanks and harnesses. Only a single pair of Marines and a few medics and droids were in the room.

Alanar placed a hand on one of the soldier's armour-plated arms and the suited figure turned sharply before saluting.

"At ease, Crewman," said the Commodore, waiting for the being (who appeared to be Human) to relax before continuing. "Two high-ups have been brought here. One is horrifyingly wounded, the other is almost catatonic. Where are they?"

"The injured one is in that tank and the catatonic is on the cot there," answered the Marine in a grating tone, pointing.

"How are they?"

"I'm no medic, Commodore, but they both appear to be in a bad way and not improving."

"Thank you, Crewman."

Alanar strode over to one of the tanks holding the gravely wounded Winn Winn still in its suit and moving only a little. The Hygran activated the intercom link within the tank.

"I am Commodore Alanar, Head of the joint Hygran-Confederation Navy mission to Second Hygra. You're aboard the Confederation swordship *Vigilant Watchman*, the ship that saved you. We'll keep you safe but I need information on something one of your Controllers gave me."

The suited figure twitched slightly, then shuddered as if in pain.

"Fo...for...forgive m...my...sllowness, Comm..o-dore," came the mechanised reply. "I ha...ve...I...am hav...having...diff...difficulty...adj...adjusting...t...to y...your...sys...systemss."

Alanar frowned.

"Why not speak normally? Our translators are functional."

"N...n...no. I c...can't...speeeak with n...n...no m...mouth"

"What?"

The Winn Winn shuddered again, more violently this time. A series of computerised sounds came instead of words. The Commodore was about to speak again when he was interrupted by a synthesised male voice.

"Apologies, Commodore," it began, "the body inside this suit has suffered significant physical and mental degradation over the years. It is wired directly into the suit, technology remarkably different to your own. There are compatibility issues."

"I see. And who am I speaking to now?"

"The integration of suit and body is so great you are speaking to neither and both. We are inseparable now."

Alanar suppressed a shudder at the thought.

"Whose body is inside the suit?"

"The body belongs to High Military Controller Shi'ke'tol'ha'then Holiva, Head of Winn Winn Imperial Military Intelligence. It would feel gratitude for your assistance if it could still feel stable emotions."

"How did they sustain such injuries and survive?"

"The High Controller was being held at an enemy interrogation and processing facility that was attached to a medical science facility. Some of the procedures performed following capture proved most damaging. His extraction was one of the primary objectives of our taskforce."

Alanar's eyes widened as the magnitude of the situation dawned on him.

"You attacked a Republic installation and brought a war criminal over our border?"

"As part of the taskforce mission, yes. We will not argue over the semantics of the words 'war criminal' and 'Republic'."

He regarded the mangled suit encasing the rotting, dissected near-corpse within for a moment. Even through all the neutral circuitry and scar tissue, the hatred of the Tardigs still burned within.

"One of your Controllers provided me with a data-package full of classified information before they died. It requires an access code to unlock to be delivered to my superiors. Do you have this key?"

"Controller Gobari is dead?"

"Unfortunately, yes. Do you have the access code?"

The being was quiet.

"High Controller, I have been asked by a member of your staff to pass classified data to my superiors. I need that access code to do so."

"Forgive our hesitation, Commodore Alanar. Controller Gobari was a Close One of the High Controller. An intense, quasi-emotional response impaired my functioning. Regarding your access codes, I am unable to provide them as long as we are in such close proximity to the enemy and its agents. My organic components will simply not allow it."

"My Chief Medical Officer tells me you have less than twenty-four hours to live."

"My organic self, perhaps. This suit will continue to store residual data for hours more. You have time, Commodore."

The Hygran sighed, frustrated.

"Alright, alright. I'll double your guard in the meantime. May I ask what the taskforce's mission was?"

"To deliver the classified data to Star Haven and assist the Confederation."

"Assist us with what?"

"I cannot say specifically, but the security of the Galaxy is at stake, Commodore. You must trust us."

"Or I could interrogate your friend over there," gestured Alanar.

"I assume you are referring to Sub-Controller Shafi? In which case, you would make little progress. The enemy has inflicted much damage on her thought cortex, rendering her catatonic."

Dammit, thought Alanar.

"Very well, High Controller. I'll do what I can to get you out of system, but my priority is to house those casualties and negotiate with the Republic."

"Then we may all pay the price for diplomacy's sake."

Alanar turned away and walked up to the marine guards.

"I want additional medical support for that tank and call in two more guards for it specifically."

"Yes, Commodore."

"Have a full squad on standby, too, and seal off this room, just in case."

"Yes, Commodore."

He nodded and strolled out, contacting Lal-ne-vo.

"Commodore?"

"How are things progressing, Captain?"

"I think it's safe to say we've got all the major areas covered and rescued the bulk of the refugees. We can begin moving back to the colony any time."

"Very good. Order Captain Thor'nek's ships to remain here and continue operations here while the rest of the ships move the casualties to Second Hygra. No doubt the Republic will want its ships back. Lay in a course and retrieve the support-ships. I'll meet you in the C3C."

Lal-ne-vo nodded and the link terminated, leaving Alanar to make his way back to the C3C. The meeting with the High Controller had greatly unnerved him. How could the Winn Winn do that to themselves? To trap oneself and violate one's body so thoroughly was abhorrent. Could they be telling the truth? What possible gain could be made from torturing someone so?

He arrived on the deck of the C3C just as the last supports began their final approach.

"Communications, get me all the departing vessels."

"Done, Sir."

"This is Commodore Alanar to the departing sections of the fleet. Prepare to jump back to Second Hygra's orbit. Once there we'll co-ordinate the offloading of survivors to the surface. Get your designated marine squads to accompany them to secure the ground strikes, too."

"Section ships are acknowledging orders."

"Last ships report ready to jump."

The Commodore stood next to Lal-ne-vo's command podium.

"Begin the countdown," he ordered.

"Jumping ships in five...four...three...two...one...jump!"

Due to the particle density within the systems, space-lane interfaces were much faster and more precise than those that made the existence of interstellar powers possible. In the space of less than thirty seconds, six ships had transited to orbit over the Hygran planet.

"Jump complete."

"Contact the colony and begin prepping for drops."

"We've managed to raise the Colony-Governor."

"Establish holographic projection."

Images of both Akshell and Morix29 appeared before him.

"Commodore," Akshell said, smiling, "you are earlier than we had expected."

"But most of the preparations are in place," added Morix. "I can connect you to traffic control and partition part of myself off to co-ordinate the operation."

"Excellent. Please do so with the Colony-Governor's permission and begin the offloading."

"If you have nothing else to do, Commodore, I would like to invite you to a dinner later today," said Akshell. "It's a bit hastily arranged, but we wanted to make you and your officers feel at home until the Republic arrives."

"Absolutely. Contact us when you need us. Alanar out."

The links died.

"Right," the Commodore said, blowing his cheeks out. "Good work everyone. Captain, if you'll excuse me, I'd like to get some rest before our dinner. I'd advise all senior staff to do likewise. Once transfers are complete, put all crew on relaxed status. We've all worked really hard today."

*   *   *

A few hours later, Alanar woke up in the cabin the ship had allocated him feeling much more refreshed. No-one had come to wake him so he assumed everything had gone smoothly. His synth-sym displayed only a few housekeeping messages. The bulk of survivors and casualties were now safely ensconced in their temporary homes. Much of the Confederation elements had deployed around the colony in stand-down mode and the times for the dinner had been delivered. It was in half an hour. Plenty time.

He threw back the bed sheets and got up. He'd been so tired that he'd only taken time to remove his coat, trousers, boots and cap. The rest he had slept in. It wasn't so bad, though. The form-hold fibres embedded in his uniform would ensure it wouldn't look creased for long.

After washing and drying his face and head he threw on the rest of his uniform, sending out several messages to the ships over Second Hygra as he did so. All available ship executive officers were to report to the surface at Government Tower and the rest of the fleet would continue orbiting as usual.

Once dressed he made his way down to the L-L bay where the Captain and Officer Mwargh Argh stood waiting next to a gunship ready to depart.

"I'm glad you could both make it," the Commodore said, thankfully.

"It's alright, Commodore," explained Mwargh Argh plainly. "Once the offloading was completed in its majority there was not much else left to do."

"Let's hope that continues to be the case. I imagine that once the Republic finally gets its act together the transition will be pretty smooth." Alanar smiled at the blunt honesty of the Kin-Sai.

The trio climbed aboard and the gunship lifted off, shooting through the bay opening and down towards the planet. Several other wasp-profiled shapes could also be seen descending rapidly from their motherships.

"How are our guests settling in, Captain? I got the message they were mostly safely down but it wasn't very descriptive."

"Well enough, I'm told, Commodore," the Talan replied. "My Marine Operations Officer informs me that they are being quiet mostly, but I ordered the separation of the officers from the lower ranks just in case they try anything."

"Very perceptive. And the crews? I assume they're enjoying the break?"

"Well, it's been a busy last few days. I'd say so, yes."

"Ah good. I'm glad I'm not being perceived as too hard a task master."

"The crews do their duty to the Confederation whether it is hard or not, Commodore," growled Mwargh Argh quietly. "It is our privilege."

Alanar nodded.

The gunship landed on one of the decks of the Government Tower within seconds of its fellows and the occupants walked towards the congregation of executive officers gathered with the welcoming committee.

From the Confederation fleet there stood: the Rigellian Captain Thor'nek and his FCO, the Human Officer Dworkin from the *Star Dragon*, Captain Lauren Shuresh and FCO Hans Schwartz, Ship-Commander Holon and his Second, Officer Anderson and the captains and FCOs from the accompanying shieldships. From the Hygran colony side there were the Colony-Governor, her subordinates and Squadron-Commander Leshlek and his own Ship-Commanders. All in full uniform it was pleasing to see, Alanar noted mentally.

His synth-sym received a ping from Morix29 as he surveyed the scene and he accepted. The bio-engineered implant projected an image of her before him.

"Good to see you again, Commodore."

"And you, Morix. We appear to be doing incredibly well."

"Indeed. I have been monitoring the transfers throughout. Our forces have performed brilliantly, but then they are Confederation."

"And Hygran, don't forget."

"You know what I mean. On that note, though, it is unfortunate our HDD counter-parts are so far out and so needed to stay there."

The Commodore thought of Navat.

"Maybe."

Akshell walked up to him and Morix expanded her presence to include the Colony-Governor.

"I'm glad you could make it, Alanar."

"Well, I never could resist a free meal," he said, grinning, "and it does make for a decent reward."

"I'm glad you see this as a job well done. Some of my people are expressing some concern at the level of armaments you're bringing into the holding areas."

Alanar chuckled.

"It's just a few security squads, Akshell. They aren't even fully armoured or armed."

The Colony-Governor cocked her head.

"I suppose you and I have very different ideas on what constitutes light arms. Then again, you are Confederation Navy."

"Trust me, Akshell. I won't keep my guns on your colony any longer than I have to."

"I hope so, Commodore. It doesn't bother me but my people get anxious with so much artillery in the streets."

Alanar suppressed a sigh as the colonials began ushering everyone inside for the event. Morix disappeared into the air, searching for a place to establish herself. Eventually, they came to a room of several tables covered in ornate cutlery. Standard etiquette for diplomatic functions began to apply. The swordship captains stuck with their Commodore, everyone else peeled off to attempt to achieve an even distribution. It worked incredibly well.
As they sat, Morix29 appeared in a specially-outfitted chair next to Alanar, looking up and grinning at him.

"Are you planning on eating?" the Commodore asked.

"I've hooked myself into the private communications grid of this building," she explained, "so in a sense I am enjoying a meal already."

"I hope it's not affecting your other work."

"Not in the slightest. My partitioned selves are monitoring everything satisfactorily, allowing me to focus my real self here."

The Commodore nodded quietly, still struggling to grasp the alien concept of 'partitioning'.

Once everyone was seated and the commotion died down, the Colony-Governor stood to make a toast.

"On behalf of the people of Second Hygra, I would like to thank the officers of the Confederation Navy and commend our own military and civilian personnel who have provided assistance of the highest quality to our Tardig and Winn Winn charges in their time of need. Let this operation strengthen the spirit of our alliance and see the casualties of the brutal conflict safe and well again. Peace, Freedom and Prosperity to all people, everywhere."

"To all people everywhere," repeated everyone in the room, joining the toast and the motto of the Confederation. Akshell sat and the feasting began.

"I have to say, Akshell, you pulled this together rather quickly."

"Well, when you live on a frontier world, you learn to keep a catering unit on twenty-four hour standby," the woman smiled back.

"Is it all from your native stock?" asked Captain Shuresh, sipping a glass of thick green liquid.

"Indeed, Captain. The survey teams spent a full decade cataloguing the planetary biota before opening the world up for colonisation. It's something of a joke amongst Second Hygrans that it took so long because they were sampling all the food potential products."

"That *is* over twice as long as standard survey work," commented Morix.

"Given the importance of this world to our species, it was vital to be very careful about testing everything to the maximum extent. Hygra has invested a lot of capital in this project," explained Leshtek. "I wish they'd been so generous with the military allotment."

"Perhaps the HDD will increase your force once operations at Nahypra have ended," suggested Captain Thor'nek. "Can't take that long to evacuate a few million settlers."

"More to the point, who had the bright idea of allowing the Wanderers to set up shop on a planet so unstable?" pointed out Shuresh. "The place was literally falling apart before they even got there."

"The Confederation Navy did issue a warning beforehand, but it cannot forcibly stop a peaceful settlement," said Morix. "Particularly if all we had in the area is a single detachment of ships."

"Hmm and now the HDD has to pick up the pieces," Leshtek quipped.

"You have help," pointed out Morix in a mock high-strung fashion. "The Far Earth and Tau-Kian police forces both sent ships."

"A few police cruisers and carriers pales in comparison to the might of the Hygran fleet."

Morix simply raised an eyebrow in response.

"In spite of our obvious deficiencies, though, we have done very well, I think," Alanar said diplomatically. "Let's hope the operation will not have to go on much longer."

"Well put," agreed Akshell. "Which reminds me, when –"

A dull roar sounded in the distance and the air seemed to vibrate momentarily. Everyone went quiet, trying to determine the source of the interruption.

"Commodore," breathed Morix sharply and quietly.

Alanar turned to the UIPE, a dark expression had fallen across her digital visage and she appeared to flicker briefly.

"What is it, Morix?"

She began to speak but was cut off and flickered again.

"Something... some-some-something is wrong. Two of my partitioned selves have gone silent."

"Explain!"

He watched as a new expression he never expected to see on the face of a UIPE unfolded: abject fear.

"I cannot feel them anymore. I have lost gunship traffic control and secure casualty oversight, both the current uplinks and their histories. It's like they were never there. Gaping holes are all that remain."

She looked directly at him.

"The network between my selves has been compromised by an external force. I am no longer a viable secure asset. Request permission to shut myself down until the situation has resolved."

"Granted."

"Commencing compete UIPE routine and sub-routine shutdown," she said mechanically."I suggest you check the secure locations and shipping records. Who knows what I've done. Shutting down."

Her image died, leaving nothing but unoccupied space in her wake and a gravely-worried Commodore.

"Alanar," Akshell pressed, putting a hand on his arm, "what is going on?"

"I've no idea," he said before standing up. "Everyone, get to your stations. We may have a security breach. Deploy full combat air patrols and lock down all sensitive –"

The explosion was deafening. In an instant all the windows shattered and everyone in the room was knocked to the ground by the concussive force of the blast. Alarms shrieked and security personnel from the local police burst into the room.

Alanar began pushing himself from the ground, looking around the ruined room. The blast must have been on a nearby floor, otherwise everyone would be dead. He saw Akshell being helped up by a guard and had barely opened his mouth to speak when another explosion sounded high above. And another. And another.

Then the burning remnants of a gunship fell past the window nearest him, its crew shrieking in agony as their craft melted and burned around them. The Tower was under attack!

"Colony-Governor," the guard reported loudly, "someone is attacking the Tower with missiles. We must evacuate to the emergency command bunker immediately!"

"Of course. Get everyone down there," she said before turning to Alanar, a long cut and streak of blood running down her left cheek. "Commodore, I think you should come with us until we find a safer way to get you back to your ships."

He nodded and they began making their way down through the building. In the time it took to reach the ECB they encountered no-one who knew what was going on. All that was known was that someone had fired on Government Tower and was continuing to do so. Synth-sym and NFI communication was ineffective in the confusion.

Once they reached the entrance of the hardened underground shelter, a Hygran male in ship-commander's uniform marched up to them and saluted. He was covered in blood and dust.

"Colony-Governor, Commodore," he began, "I'm glad you're alright."

"Thank you, Ship-Commander Hegack," Akshell said. "What's going on?"

Hegack motioned them inside where chaos appeared to reign supreme. Every one of the stations was occupied by constantly-speaking operators who, in turn, were bellowed at by frantic officers.

"We still have no clear idea. Only that the holding areas for the battle casualties have been the sites of some altercations with the Navy security forces since the attack on the Tower began."

"What about the Navy ships in orbit?" demanded Alanar, worriedly.

"Still in orbit, but communication has been disrupted somehow. We're trying to set up a remote link now via the OTR, but our priority is locating and stopping those missiles."

"I see. In which case I'll need a station to head up the effort from," said the Commodore. "I must contact my fleet."

"Very well, Sir. This way."

He was quickly led to a station to begin the process of trying to contact the fleet. Though focused on the task at hand, he could not help but worry about Morix29. If she had been compromised there was a good chance the operation as a whole lay open to further cybernetic attack. What was going on up there?

"Commodore, may I be of assistance?" asked Lal-ne-vo.

"If you know anything about communication-ware, yes. How are the others?"

"They're helping treat the wounded and awaiting further orders."

Alanar smiled. You could always count on a Navy officer to be where they were needed.

"Have you tried the regular channels?" asked the Talan, staring at the screen.

"Yes. They are all scrambled or non-functional."

"Hmm...try broadcasting to the support craft on their wavelengths. They can route a signal to the ships."

Alanar tapped a few keys.

"Done," he said and began broadcasting. "This is Commodore Alanar to any Confederation ship in orbit of Second Hygra. Do you read me?"

The console was briefly silent but then crackled to life.

"This is gunship 22-Alpha responding. It's good to hear from you, Commodore. Are you alright?"

"Negative, 22-Alpha. The colony is under fire from inside. We believe the casualties held here have overpowered their guards and begun fighting. I need you to serve as a relay to the fleet and get every available Marine on the ground now before this gets completely out of hand."

"Communications are patchy up here, too, I'm afraid, Sir. It may take some time to –"

"Switch to support craft channels and call those inside the hangars," interrupted Lal-ne-vo.

"Roger that. Activating uplink and switching over. Any further orders, Commodore?"

"Locate the enemy and dispatch Marines. That is all. Alanar out."

The link terminated. Another detonation thrummed overhead.

"We have a new report," Hegack hollered and the room quietened significantly.

"Those Tardigs and Winn Winn held on the surface have escaped from every holding location, overpowered their guards, obtained heavy Confederation Navy weapons and freed their officers. They are now advancing on each other and this location. Local security is responding but with minimal effect. Casualties are heavy."

"Right now I need every available being who can fire a gun to assist in the defence of this sector while we wait for the Navy reinforcements to arrive. Weapons will be distributed as you leave."

He saluted and approached the Colony-Governor, motioning Alanar over.

"I need numbers of troops, weapons and capabilities if we are to have any hope of defending this place," the Ship-Commander requested.

"Before she went offline my second-in-command noted that key parts of her matrix had been corrupted – possibly infiltrated," admitted Alanar. "Any figures I could give aren't necessarily reliable. I didn't even know we had heavy weaponry down here until it was reported. My best guess is that only several thousand combatants comprise each side."

"How can they be making such progress, then? They've already taken three entire districts!"

"If the Winn Winn have access to their formsuits and the Tardigs can use their battle armour, then your own police won't stand a chance. Neither will your military troopers. The defence of hardened positions must be our first priority until my Marines arrive."

There was a shriek as a high-speed projectile ripped the air and a crash when it ploughed into the ground moments later.

"Why are they targeting the Tower and not just each other?" Akshell wondered. "I thought they'd be too busy exacting revenge."

"The bunker!" realised Hegack and Alanar simultaneously.

"It contains the locations of every armoury and hardpoint in the colony," the Ship-Commander went on, "if they take it, they'll exercise complete control."

The colour drained away from Akshell's face at the thought.

"Commodore, you must get back to your fleet and organise support," she insisted. "We'll stick here and fend them off as best we can until you do."

He looked at her speechless.

"There's a government airfield at Pointersfield, less than two kilometres from here," Hegack said briskly, handing him a pistol and sending an access code to his synth-sym. "Use this to access one of the shuttles."

Alanar accepted both.

"Thank you, Ship-Commander. I will come back for all of you. My officers are at your disposal."

"Good luck!"

The two military men saluted one another. Alanar looked grimly at Akshell.

"Go," she mouthed and he took off out of the room.

Outside the chaos was undiminished. Every few moments, gun or shell fire would roll through the air followed by screams, cries and explosions. Huge columns of smoke had begun to emerge from clusters of burning buildings. Panicked colonists ran through the streets, desperately trying to escape the carnage that had suddenly been inflicted upon them.

In the time it took to reach the airfield, a flat area kept clear for that exact purpose, most of the aircraft had already departed, or at least appeared to have done so. But several unarmed shuttles were left on the open ground and were being prepped for operations. Alanar didn't rate the chances of the departed craft very highly. He ran over to a guard at the entrance.

"I'm the Confederation Navy Commodore with the fleet in orbit and I need access to a shuttle to get up there," he said, datavising his credentials.

"Of course, Sir," the guard replied. "This way."

They approached the nearest shuttle and explained the situation to the head of the prep team.

"Running away from the mess you made, are you?" sniped the female Hygran. "Use your own damn birds, you coward!"

"What?!"

"You heard me. Blasted Confederation. This is all your fault!"

"I need a shuttle to contact my fleet and bring down support. Please –"

"Clear off!"

"Communications are down. I need –"

She swung for him and he deflected the blow with ease, drawing his pistol and holding it an inch from her face.

"Get me a plane – now!"

She silently motioned to the ground team who began disconnecting the prep equipment. Two minutes later Alanar was in the cockpit and the shuttle was taking to the skies over the mega-city. As the view of the sprawl increased he could see the areas embroiled in conflict. Judging by the feats being performed by the figures in the distance, the two sides had indeed gained access to their powered armour and had brought their conflict to the streets of Second Hygra.

The shuttle shot through the clouds and into the upper atmosphere. As soon as the craft had entered space he became aware of a signal being broadcast at his ship and he tuned in.

"Attention, Hygran shuttle. This is Communications Officer She'lok aboard the *Vigilant Watchman*. Identify yourself and state your intent. There is a class C conflict zone."

"This is Commodore Alanar requesting permission to land and a sit-rep," he replied.

There was a pause.

"Permission granted. We have managed to purge the programme disrupting communications for the most part, but contact with the surface is still being blocked by a similar programme. Acting Captain Roaragh is organising a Marine force to deal with the situation on the ground supported by our entire support craft complement. It should be departing within the hour."

"Is there any way to hurry it along?"

"The entire command staff is gone, Commodore. We are also struggling to co-ordinate in the continuing presence of the communications blocker elements we've not purged yet."

"I see. I will assist ship-side. We need boots on the ground asap."

The shuttle touched down shortly after. As Alanar climbed out, the scene that presented itself made it obvious that a military operation was imminent. Marines and pilots rushed around alongside engineers, loading up their craft and combat suits with more weaponry than was usual for normal operations. It struck him that this would be the Navy's first real combat mission. Shots would actually be fired in anger for the first time since the founding of the Confederation. Not quite the honour he wanted in this mission, he thought as he headed to the C3C.

The hardened room was in a state of some chaos when he got there, nothing new in the last hour or so. He caught the eye of a Kin-Sai at the command podium.

"Acting Captain Roaragh, it's good to be back aboard."

The huge alien snapped to attention.

"Commodore, I'm glad you're safe."

"Thank you, but this is far from over. What have you got ready to go?"

"About a third of our units report ready to deploy. I wanted to wait until we were at full readiness –"

"Forget it. Tell them to deploy now and we'll feed the rest in as they come online."

"Our target?"

"Secure the emergency command bunker area and establish a link with the fleet isolated from local communications. Once we secure that then we can think about restoring order to the rest of the colony."

"Yes, Commodore."

It then occurred to him that the security of the system at large might be in jeopardy. More fire-power may be needed.

"What about our Hygran picket forces and long-range communications?"

The Acting Captain checked her instruments on the command podium before nodding back to the Hygran.

"We've lost contact with the pickets but they still show up on –"

The podium buzzed on alert.

"The *Shamsha* just dropped off scanners now."

"What?!" exclaimed Alanar. "Sensor Analysis report!"

"No evidence of evasive manoeuvres or contact with the other picket- ships, Commodore. It's almost like they went to stealth mode but HDD light-cruisers aren't equipped for that."

Alanar ran an inventory through his synth-sym. No, the *Shamsha* wasn't designed for clandestine ops. Perhaps it had been quickly isolated and destroyed. That implied a larger Winn Winn force was coming for its people. They may even have engineered the whole situation on the colony as cover to rescue their high-ranking officers. Definitely time to call the cavalry in.

"I'll assume long-range communications are disrupted?" he asked.

"For now, but engineering is working on it! They believe it should be functioning within a half hour. Probably less."

"Right, as soon as LRCs are restored I want you to contact Admiral Kisugi and request the immediate assistance of the support squadron on standby. We could be looking at a massive border breach. See if you can get hold of Tardig Border Command and recommend they reinforce this sector but not to cross into our space. I won't have a chaotic fire-fight if this escalates. Order our pickets to high alert and to watch for any incoming hostiles. I'll be interrogating our Winn Winn guests onboard here. I want to know exactly what is going on down there."

He turned to march off the C3C.

"What of the *Shamsha*, Commodore?"

Alanar looked at the display of the entire system, specifically the place where *Shamsha* had last been sighted. If there were survivors, or if something sinister was going on, he couldn't leave them out there.

"Closest ship?"

"The shieldship *Pride of Kanassit*, attached to *Star Dragon's* escort."

"Once its marines are offloaded, transfer command of them here and despatch it to investigate and patrol until communications are restored."

"Yes, Commodore."

He resumed his march toward where the High Military Controller was being held. It occurred to him that the removal of the majority of the marine complement to the surface may have left the containment area woefully short-staffed and guarded, but while fully-armed and armoured Winn Winn might trounce Hygran police staff, he didn't rate a group of walking wounded against Navy Marines very highly.

Thankfully, the four guards he had ordered to the room had remained unmolested in their duty, only briefly regarding him as he rolled up to the tank and motioned the attendee bots and medics away with a loud, "Clear the deck!"

Once they had left, he rounded on the tank. Its occupant had noticeably degraded since they had last spoken.

"I have no time for misdirection and non-answers this time, High Controller," the Commodore began. "Lives are at stake on Second Hygra and I need to know the exact capabilities of your ground forces, the fleet you have about to attack us and how you have managed to penetrate our computer systems – now!"

"I do not understand, Commodore," it began after a long pause. "We have no wish to attack either Hygra or the Confederation Navy. Our capabilities would not allow it even if we wanted to."

"Bullshit! Your troops are on the colony as we speak, razing the place to the ground with Confederation weapons you hijacked. The Tardigs appear to be engaging them as we speak. Is this some sort of ruse for us to fall into so you can be rescued? Because, rest assured, there is no chance of you surviving a battle with the Confederation Navy."

"Commodore Alanar, this entity has willingly placed itself in your charge for delivery to Navy Command. We do not wish rescue. There is no rescue to come."

"Then why have you attacked and destroyed a Hygran light-cruiser? Why are you attacking the colony? Why are your viruses in our mainframe? Damn it, High Controller, I have no time for this. The chaos must end."

"Will you give this entity access to your data-stream?"

"Why?"

"Understand us, Commodore. We are not responsible for what you think we are on Second Hygra, but if what is happening is what we suspect it is, then you could be in grave danger."

"From what?"

"We cannot say without further information."

"And I can't give you access without you giving me more," half-yelled Alanar.

The High Controller – or what remained of it sealed in that eviscerated monstrosity – shuddered violently and the tank reported a drop in the bio-signs of the being. They recovered quickly but it was a disturbing change.

"The data-stream, Commodore. Please."

This was going nowhere. Yet the urgency in the High Controller's tone gave him a gut feeling that perhaps some trust and give may yield some results.

The Commodore took a breath.

"You'll get the files covering the incident from its beginning until now and no live access. Then you will tell me exactly what is going on," he conceded, preparing the information in his synth-sym.

"Very well, but we will need time to assess the data provided," the Winn Winn agreed after a pause.

"How long?"

"Perhaps, half an hour. No more."

"You have that long and that's it. If I don't get what I want, I will not hesitate to authorise lethal force against all combatants involved – with extreme prejudice."

"Please, Commodore!" he responded, a new urgency filling the air. "Only restrain them if indeed they are attacking. You have no idea how precious they are."

Several awkward moments passed. Alanar turned away.

"Half an hour, High Controller, or things will get bloody," he declared and then left, opening a private channel to the Acting Captain as he did so.

"Yes, Commodore?"

"Just a reminder to stress the use of non-lethal restraining methods by our Marines where possible. At least until I give orders otherwise."

"Very good, Commodore. The *Pride of Kanassit* has also just left on its mission."

"Keep an eye on it, Acting Captain. I don't want to lose another ship. How is the landing operation progressing"

"The first wave is on the ground now and has made contact with the Navy and HDD officers at the ECB. Our officers are being airlifted now."

"Excellent! Do we have full air coverage and supremacy?"

"Confederation military communications on the ground with our units have been re-established and we are working on the HDD nets now. Full cohesion within the hour, but effectively we have control."

"Keep working at it. Offer the colonial government evacuation options. I'll join you on the deck shortly."

The C3C had calmed noticeably, even with the presence of real-time live feeds to the landing site marines and a virtual tactical display of the combat zone. From the occasional reports broadcast over the PA it appeared good progress was being made.

"This is squad VW227CNM to command. We have secured point 2110. Five squids down."

"SD164CNM here. Lizards in retreat from the Arsik Buildings."

"Mobile Ground Command general report: engagements increasing but general retreats where hostiles are not engaging each other."

"What is happening where they are?" asked the Commodore of the Acting Captain.

"It's pretty fierce, Commodore. It would seem they are intent on murdering each other."

They looked at the displays. It appeared the Winn Winn and Tardigs were colliding in three key areas and were in the process of razing them to the ground. So much hatred. It was unimaginable within the Confederation.

"Any word on civilian causalities yet?"

"Nothing concrete, but it looks to be lower than we initially thought. After the confusion at the start of the incident, most Hygrans evacuated quickly once they realised what was happening. Some pockets are still trapped but no reports of hostages being taken."

"And the local HDD forces and police?"

"The defence cutters are holding position under the subsidiary protocol. No certain word of the planet-side movements, though the scattered data we have picked up shows no serious resistance being mounted and relatively minimal casualties."

"The AIs have suggested that the attacks on the Government Tower and local defence installations were only meant to cripple allied responses while they attacked each other."

"Makes sense. They've been going at it for a long time. What about the possibility that this is a diversion to allow a rescue of the High Controller?" asked Alanar.

"We have considered this and suggest it is the most likely probability. Given the Winn Winn ability to compromise UIPE partitioning and other systems, it is highly likely they will have a method of penetrating other areas, too," commented the featureless AI image of the *Vigilant Watchman* which had super-imposed itself on the live-feed display.

It made no recommendations, though. Alanar found himself missing the presence of Morix29. He could still make decisions, but having her here to tweak and support them would help, even if it was just his confidence.

"Nothing yet on the *Shamsha*?" he asked and a screen switched to the system display where the *Pride of Kanassit* could be seen clearly conducting its search.

"Not as of yet, Commodore."

In a way, some good news could be taken from that. If the *Pride* was there and there was no sign of combat, then the forces which had taken out *Shamsha* either hadn't made it through the breach or were very small. Still, that was no reason to let their guard down.

"Signal the fleet. The moment any Winn Winn vessel shows up on close-range sensors, I want it targeted and interrogated. The second hostile action occurs, disable it."

"Yes, Commodore."

"AI, what could the Winn Winn have used to take out the *Shamsha*?"

"Unknown. Similar results have been yielded as to how they have achieved the other disruptions. Highest possibilities suggest a ranged weapon that suppresses any trace elements after use – two hundred and fourteen such weapons could be modified to fit such a profile."

Nothing about this made any sense. The Winn Winn insurgency was, the strategic consensus said, nowhere near as powerful as it had been. They should not have the abilities they appeared to display here. Yet they did. They had nothing to gain from attacking the Confederation due to its vast firepower. Yet they did. Sharing information with the Navy would yield no results, given that it could not intervene. Yet they did.

Everything pointed to this being an insurgency operation, but its objectives were unclear to the point of appearing non-existent or conflicting to the point of confusion.

"I'd like a sit-rep on the status of Morix29."

"The UIPE Morix29 is still inactive within Second Hygra and *Vigilant Watchman's* networks. The further status of the elements on Second Hygra is impossible to ascertain due to communications difficulties; core elements are mostly ship-side and scans indicate they are free from external influence."

"Wake her up, then. Shield the areas she occupies. Let's be safe."

"Yes, Commodore. Accessing and reactivating the UIPE routines. Erecting firewalls and shielding. Routines —"

"— established. UIPE functioning restored," interrupted Morix, her hologram materialising before them. "Well...mostly, anyway."

"Thanks for small mercies," sighed Alanar. "Any insights into this mess?"

"I'm analysing the available data now. It's hard without access to Second Hygra's networks."

"It's for your own safety, Morix."

She simply nodded and closed her holographic eyes, focusing. It took almost a full minute for her to run through everything. The loss of the partitions must have compromised her functionality badly.

"Commodore, we may have a problem far bigger than it might initially appear," the UIPE began. "The Winn Winn could not have compromised my matrices without the help of another entity like myself. As near as I'm aware, they've never had possession of such technology and an external construct would have to willingly wish to do so. Even then, such a violation is difficult to perpetrate stealthily."

"But who would want to help the Insurgency and risk the wrath of the Republic?" asked Roaragh.

"There is another possibility, but I am hesitant to point it out. The implications are not great."

"Go on," encouraged Alanar.

"The Tardig Republic has the technology to create UIPE-like constructs," she said simply.

Alanar would have laughed had the situation not been so serious.

"What possible reason could the Republic have to start a conflict on a Confederation aligned world? They are our allies!"

"I am not privy to Republic strategic planning, Commodore, but the fact remains they have the capability."

"Capability does not translate to intent," argued the Hygran.

The truth was, though, this new information was unsettling to say the least. The Republic had saved the Confederation from a costly war by effectively destroying the Winn Winn nation. They were close allies. The prospect of hostile intent on their part was unthinkable, yet something about this entire affair had unsettled him almost from the outset: the sheer lack of response from the Tardigs. Military bureaucracy could only partially explain it. But the question remained: why would the Republic initiate hostile action against the Confederation?

"Long-range communications are back up and running, Commodore," reported the Communications Officer.

"Signal Admiral Kisugi and Tardig Border Control," ordered Alanar.

"Commodore –" started Morix.

"I'm sorry, but I just cannot believe the Republic is responsible for this, Morix. Even if they are, we'll find out for certain once this is all over and an investigation is launched."

The UIPE remained silent after that. Alanar nodded at the Communications Officer pointedly, ensuring the order was followed.

"Marines are near fully deployed or in transit, Commodore," Roaragh noted," and the officer gunships are linking up with their escorts. Estimated time of arrival is five minutes and counting."

"And the colonial government?"

"Only Squadron-Commander Leshtek is en route."

"What?!" demanded Alanar, his expression darkening further.

"Colony-Governor Akshell and the rest of the local military and government staff have opted to remain behind to personally oversee the situation."

He admired the courage but questioned the wisdom of staying in a war zone. In any case, the offer had been made and rejected. He had to focus on the primary task of re-securing the colony.

"Alright, continue the operation. Sit-rep for the colony?"

"MGC is setting up a firewall around the combat zone with the new arrivals. Several key locations have been taken, but there is now severe fighting and damage in the main engagement zones," reported Mwargh Argh.

"Damn. Are our aerial ops having any effects?"

"MGC hasn't vectored in any fighters yet. They believe the effects would be counter-productive to the infrastructure and operation."

Alanar ran through his head for solutions or any way to assist his ground forces. None were forthcoming. Unless...

"Morix, how are your communications infiltration skills?"

"Second to none."

He looked at a screen as it showed Marines storming one building and unloading suppressing fire into another.

"Think you can hack their communications systems?"

"I'll download to MGC and assist. At least we can get an idea of numbers."

"Al," ordered the Commodore, "allow the UIPE access to MGC. And Morix, be safe out there."

"Yes, Commodore," came the reply as Morix flared way.

He clasped both pairs of hands behind his back and positioned himself before the three screens. All of this had got out of hand so quickly. Even once the planet was under control they still had to locate *Shamsha*, the culprits and repair the damage to the mega-city.

Combat in interstellar warfare was just the relatively easy beginning. It was why so few wars were fought by multi-planetary powers over single worlds; even fewer over many. The Centaurian Civil War and the Winn Winn-Tardig Conflict were exceptions in galactic history. The resources and lives they cost were terrifyingly ruinous.

"What's the estimated time of arrival on Kisugi's squadron?"

The equipment those ships carried would be vital for the rebuilding.

"Under an hour, we estimate, Commodore."

An internal clock triggered by his synth-sym alerted him to the need to re-interview the High Controller.

"Alert me when they arrive. I need to have a chat with –"

Another alert sounded. This one very loud and for all to hear. A proximity alarm.

"Report!"

On the strategic system screen at the area near the *Pride of Kanassit*, markers for exit points appeared. Others began showing up around the edge of the system.

"Multiple EPs all over the picket zone. Count twelve – thirteen – still increasing. Over a hundred now."

"Identity?"

"Nothing confirmed yet."

"Count at three hundred. Still rising."

"These aren't ours," commented the acting captain.

As the scene unfolded, more EPs began appearing inside the picket. Near the colony.

"God." someone breathed quietly.

"Get me a direct line to the *Pride of Kanassit* – now!" demanded Alanar. "I want images of those ships, profiles – the works."

"Count now at over..." the sensor analysis officer trailed off.

"What is the count?" yelled the Hygran.

There was an audible gulp.

"Over a thousand, Commodore."

"Shit!"

"Profiles coming in now. Detecting variances in new emergences. Looks like a full fleet with supports, capital ships, carriers. Running them through the data-base now."

The wait lasted forever.

"Profiles identified. It's a Tardig Republic formation!"

"On this side of the border?"

"There must be some kind of mistake."

"Hail the closest vessel," offered Alanar, before chaos could claim his C3C.

"They're hailing us," reported the Communications Officer.

"Holo them."

A new hologram flared before him. It took the form of a nine-foot tall Tardig standing on two hind legs, supported by a long tail that extended out the back of a thick scaly torso which possessed two massive muscular arms. A lizard-like head with a sharp avian beak and two forward-facing eyes looked over, ignoring him.

It was encased almost entirely in black, smooth, featureless armour used by all Tardig military personnel with no distinguishing features. Based on the authority it projected through its body language though, Alanar guessed this was a taskforce or fleet Commander.

It began moving its jaws and the translator kicked in.

"This is Tardig Republic Naval Assault Group five seven seven attached to the 22nd Assault Fleet, Group Leader Ssslakcha Thimosss the Ninth to All People's Confederation Navy and Hygran Defence Directorate personnel in the Second Hygra system.

"As of this moment the Second Hygra star system and colony are under Republic jurisdiction and administration. Cease your operations against Republic ground forces and stand down. Your ships will be boarded and interned, as will your crews. All Winn Winn insurgents will be turned in. Any resistance will be met with maximum force. We await a reply from your commanding officers. You have five Confederation standard minutes to comply."

The hologram flared away leaving the C3C in silence.

So many questions. So little time. Too many ships. But through it all Alanar recognised his goals.

"Call back the pickets and *Star Dragon* detachment, and assume a defensive position over the colony," he began. "Standard pattern five."

"Commodore," warned Sensors, "the Republic has surrounded our pickets. If they try to jump –"

"– they'll be blown out of the sky." Great, he thought, staring at the screens, the fate of the fleet and colony weighing on him heavily.

"Contact the source of that transmission. Let's see if we can talk."

"Channel open."

"This is Confederation Taskforce Commodore Alanar to Group Leader Ssslakcha Thimosss the Ninth. We are currently on a mission of mercy to assist your people and we're holding them on the colony. If you are here to reclaim them then –"

"We are not here to rescue survivors. We are here to claim this system," came the stern faceless reply. "Will you surrender or not? You have four minutes."

"Cut the link," he ordered, now realising his oath to defend the Confederation.

"Battle stations! Re-orient our fighters to face the Republic ships. Recall the pickets."

Klaxons rang out on every ship as the fleet began to move.

"Tardigs are targeting pickets and moving inwards."

"We're too spread out!"

"More EPs opening at close range."

"They're firing!"

Missiles, projectiles, lasers, torpedoes and bombs began raining down on the picket ships. The smaller Hygran ships never stood a chance."

"We've lost two of the destroyers. All pickets report heavy fire."

"Picking up dozens of EPs. Looks like a transport flotilla and escorts. Wait! Identifying battlecruiser profiles, too."

"Concentrate fire on those battlecruisers. Fighters on the smaller ships."

"EPs above and below. Strike cruisers and frigates. They're targeting the support ships!"

"Missiles launching."

Spreads of thousands of guided missiles slid out of their bays and batteries and into space. Seconds later they found their targets, which were either executing sluggish evasive manoeuvres or caught completely off-guard.

"Birds are dropping like flies."

"Point defences to cover fire the supports," ordered Alanar. "IBLs on those new forces."

Finally, the Confederation Navy responded, its ships sending long blue ion beam lasers at the strike-cruisers and attack frigates, slicing up to four in half at a time. Small explosive pellets and missiles began intercepting the incoming enemy missiles, and large shells were sent flying at the lumbering battlecruisers. The big ships wasted little time in sending their own response, but they were each under a fifth of the size of a shieldship. It would take more to out-match the huge, advanced Confederation vessels, but the Republic still had plenty of ships.

"Our remaining pickets are reporting in. Only the remaining light-cruiser and destroyers appear to have made it"

"Status?"

"Heavily damaged, Commodore."

"Get them inside our defensive fire shell and co-ordinate their fire with ours."

"One of the defence cutters is taking heavy fire."

"Get cover from the nearest shieldship. Get the officers aboard asap."

"Commodore, we lost contact with the officer gunship transports at the start of the engagement. A lot of our gunships are off the grid right now."

" What about those transports?"

"Most are closing on the OTR. Looks like they're going to use it to land forces on the surface."

"How many main support struts does it have?"

"Just the one in the mega-city but the structure is pretty flimsy."

"Contact our ground forces. Tell them to be ready to blow the moorings on my order."

Mwargh Argh looked up, deeply concerned.

"Commodore, the strut is in a densely-populated area. Casualties will be massive."

"Have the Marines evacuate as many civilians as possible, but the primary objective is to prepare that OTR for destruction," Alanar added without taking his eyes off the displays. More Republic ships were arriving all the time. If he didn't think of something soon, the Confederation and its allies would be over-run.

A new icon appeared on the strategic display in orbit of the colony. *Pride of Kanassit* had survived.

"Status of the *Pride*?" he enquired.

"It's suffered moderate upper hull damage, mostly from missile strikes."

"Order it to join our main battle line."

The Navy was going to have to do all the leg work now. HDD ships were not designed to take on a Galactic military force. Of course, neither were the minds of the Confederation crews. Alanar still couldn't believe what was happening here. The Republic was invading Confederation space. This was impossible. It had to be a rogue force. A terrorist attack. Something. Anything.

A jolt from a shell that had broken through the point defence barrage drew him out of his stupor. A dozen more battlecruisers had followed the *Pride* to the colony.

"Transports are offloading troops to the OTR star-side hub," reported SAO. "More are moving for a direct landing."

Another impact vibrated the ship.

"What's our air coverage like?" Alanar asked the Acting Captain.

"Planet side is still a hundred percent, but it's only a fraction of our original complement and that will go down once those ships get through the atmosphere and deploy their own support.

"And up here? What can we send down to help?"

There was a pause. Too long.

"What is our coverage, Acting Captain?!"

"We lost eighty-five percent of our coverage in the opening wave of the attack. The rest are scattered and evasive. We cannot co-ordinate ground-air support."

An attack frigate blossomed into a fireball on the live screen as another shell slammed into a destroyer and a missile salvo tore up a section of *Star Dragon's* armour. The Commodore looked at the C3C crew, valiantly working to save what remained of the battered defenders.

"Send this message on all available bands and channels," he began, addressing the Communications Officer. "Message begins: to all available Confederation aligned combat craft, this is Confederation Navy Fleet. Second Hygra under attack by massive Tardig Republic military force. Requesting all available assistance in reporting or repulsing the invasion. This is not a drill. Repeat! Not a drill. Message ends."

The Communications Officer nodded as it broadcast.

"Order the Marines to blow the OTR moorings and then execute Plan: Gladio. Signal all ships: fast land all supports and jump at will to the Shanzi Comet. We'll regroup and counter-attack from there."

"Sir–" began Roaragh, protesting.

"I don't want to hear it! Follow your orders!"

An eerie silence, punctuated by the vibrations of impacts, descended as the C3C staff realised they were abandoning the colony orbit to the invader after only minutes of fighting. But to stay would have been suicide. The strategy display showed the Tardigs pushing further into the system in rapidly-increasing numbers.

With luck, blowing the OTR would stall the invasion long enough for the ground forces to set up defensive positions and hide while the fleet section came up with a way to disrupt the assault. Even with only a few ships, the Confederation unit was still a highly-damaging force to be reckoned with. Shanzi was far enough out of the way that they should be alright. At the worst they could wait until Admiral Kisugi's squadron arrived.

"Commodore," reported the Communications Officer, "I have the Colony-Governor and the temporary Squadron-Commander hailing us."

"Put them up on holo, Officer." Alanar couldn't help but think this wasn't going to be good as both figures shimmered into existence before him.

"Commodore Alanar," hollered the temporary Squad-Commander Hegack. "You cannot abandon orbit. The colony will fall!"

"Alanar, your troops are moving to blow up the OTR mooring. That could kill hundreds of people! And what is this about you leaving?!"

"We are executing a tactical withdrawal in the face of overwhelming opposition. There is no alternative. If the OTR is left intact more people will die."

Akshell's expression darkened.

"I'm sorry, Commodore, but I cannot allow the OTR to be destroyed, no matter what we are facing."

"And I will not abandon my post," added the acting Squadron-Commander.

"Need I remind you both that we are up against the Tardig Republic military here?" argued Alanar, struggling to keep his cool as more shells rained down on the hull armour and the point defences struggled to fend off missile salvos. "We can either flee and counter-attack later, or stay and die. Much as I'd like to think I can take on an entire attack force, I know I can't do it."

There was a pause as a detonation shook wherever Akshell was holed up and was distracted before turning back to the imager.

"The Republic?" she demanded, incredulously. "Damn it! I knew those bastards were up to something. Give me a little more time to evacuate the damage zone, Commodore, and you can blow the moorings. Acting Squadron-Commander, follow your orders."

"You have until we jump, Akshell. We cannot let those troops land, but we will come back for you."

"You better, Commodore – or I'll have your balls!"

The images died.

"Contact Morix29 and evacuate her from the surface," he ordered.

The UIPE could not be allowed to be captured or compromised again. Hopefully, she'd have some ideas on how to resolve this mess.

A new alarm sounded and one of the displays switched to a layout of the ship. One of its sections was highlighted in red.

"Hull armour breach! Dispatching repair crews and bots to affected areas."

"Casualties?" asked the acting captain.

"Hard to tell. Looks like a missile strike. If so, then everyone in the explosive and concussive blast zones won't have made it."

The Hygran sighed hard. This was going south far too quickly.

"Seal it off. We'll address it once we've jumped," Roaragh ordered.

Space around the engagement was rapidly filling up with the debris and detritus of half-destroyed and crippled war machines. Bodies of crew members who had survived venting and explosive decompression spasmed violently from death throws and exposure to live weaponry. Splintered, smouldering and charred hulks drifted lifelessly in the light of the battle and the colony below. All around more and more death and destruction poured out into the void. Every passing minute brought more ships out into the fray, adding to the cloud of violence swamping Second Hygra. The system was burning.

"All surviving supports are aboard. SLIDE is cycled up."

"Good! Now all we need is –"

Morix flared into existence before him.

"I am here, Commodore," she reported.

"All ships report ready to jump."

"Signal the Colony-Governor: blow the moorings."

"Signal sent."

"Jump!"

One by one, within seconds of each other, the survivors of the Confederation-Hygran fleet opened and entered entry points. As the *Vigilant* passed into stringspace, Alanar saw warships and transports begin descending through the atmosphere. For several long moments, the Commodore was seized with a sense of utter helplessness before the might of the invasion force he was facing. It was replaced with a new sense of focus as the view became that of stringspace.

Seconds later, the fleet emerged in the tail of the Shanzi comet currently skirting the edge of the system. The sensor returns showed the immediate area was clear of Tardig ships, though several groups were showing up at extreme range. With any luck the cometary debris and radiation, along with the unlikely repositioning of the fleet there, would give them enough cover to come up with a plan.

"Assume defence formation five and keep within the comet tail zone," Alanar ordered. "I want a report from every ship: weapons and support craft load-outs, casualty and damage reports, and combat readiness. Morix, join me in the captain's office."

As he moved to leave, the Communications Officer cut across his path, holding a report and a dismayed expression.

"I'm sorry, Commodore," the Officer said quietly, handing over the report, "but of all the support craft that made it, none held any of the command staff."

The report listed all of the captains and FCOs as missing in action, suspected killed in action.

He knew what it meant. They were all dead. The room felt like it was tilting as he dealt with the shock of the revelation.

"Than...Thank you, Officer. Now resume your station. Acting Captain, with me, please."

The trio quickly assembled in Lal-ne-vo's office with its various flora and fauna. All seemed quiet and drab, as though all the organisms had sensed the end of their caretaker. Alanar shared his news.

"... and so Acting Captain, I'm giving you and your counter-parts throughout the fleet immediate battle-field promotions."

Roaragh saluted sharply.

"But where to go from here?" Morix wondered aloud. "The Republic has seized the system and the colony will be taken shortly."

"We wait for Admiral Kisugi's forces to arrive and launch an all-out counter-strike," suggested Roaragh. "It's the safest option with our fleet so badly outnumbered and damaged."

"That works on the assumption the squadron or any help will arrive at all," the UIPE pointed out. "For all we know it's not just Second Hygra being seized here. The entire Confederation could be under attack."

"Don't be ridiculous! Such an operation would require firepower and logistical support on an impossible scale. This has got to be a rogue operation by some faction trying to stop the spread of the Winn Winn Insurgency. The Republic is our ally!"

"And yet its ships and troops are swamping this system."

"Arguing over the who, how and why can take place once we work out our next course of action," Alanar decided. "What matters right now is what we do now. I'm tempted to withdraw to one of our old battlestations left over from the disputes with the Winn Winn back in the day. We'll be safe there."

"Unless the Tardigs have hit them, too," Morix put in. "The fact is we do not know the nature of the attacks. I recommend withdrawing to a planet unlikely to be at the top of their list of targets."

"What about those people on the colony?" asked Roaragh. "We can't just leave them there. Even with the Plan Gladio protocols in effect they cannot hold out forever.

"We cannot risk this fleet in a pointless action that could well kill everyone taking part."

"Enough," said Alanar, quietly. "We need to assess what the enemy is doing. Monitor their progress around the system. It's a space-lane step-over point. If this is a Confederation-wide attack, then the main force will run its ships through here. Try and contact the marines and work out a way to disrupt enemy operations or evacuate our forces. Confer with the other captains until I get back."

"Where are you going?" asked the other two simultaneously.

"To get answers," the Commodore replied, heading to a part of the ship he visited all too frequently of late.

On his way there Morix flared into existence before him, a curious expression on her virtual visage.

"Where *are* you going?"

"Shouldn't you be –"

"Participating," she cut in knowingly. "Stop being evasive."

"Start following your orders!"

"I am, but unlike you I can multi-task effectively."

"Even if I wanted to share this with you, I'm not sure I could," Alanar confessed. "Even I don't have all the details."

"And a near-dead, half-destroyed mess like the High Controller does?"

The Commodore raised an eyebrow.

"I have the combined wisdom of centuries of civilisation and a near-infinitely adaptable design. I am not an idiot."

"I know, Morix. As I said, I cannot talk about it. At least, not yet."

"May I at least know why?"

"I was told to trust none of my subordinates."

Now it was the UIPE's turn to raise an eyebrow.

"By a terrorist?"

"Your partitions were compromised. Though how the High Controller could have known that I've no idea."
They arrived at the entrance to the holding room.

"If anything relevant comes out I'll let you know. Talk to the captains. Come up with something."

Morix nodded and flared away while he datavise d the door open, striding briskly towards the tank.

"I want answers, High Controller, and I want them now. Why the Tardig military has seized this system, is one of the first things I want to know."

"May we enquire as to the designation of the formation?" the floating figure requested after a pause.

"Assault group five five seven with the 22nd Assault Fleet."

The High Controller hung forlornly in its suit for another long moment.

"Then it has already begun. We are too late, or perhaps...we are sorry, Commodore, our rush to warn the Confederation of the coming threat may have inadvertently triggered it prematurely."

"What are you talking about?!"

"We cannot explain it well through words. It is the death cry of an entire species. Please enable us to internally project into your implants."

Alanar did so with a thought, erecting fire-walls in the same moment. He would not be caught off-guard again.

"You have access."

"Very well."

There was a rush of images in his mindscape. Galaxies, nebulae, star systems, planets, fleets of warships of all shapes and sizes, and eventually a single planet of varying shades of turquoise, bathed in the light of an orange star, floated below him. A few metres away hung a Winn Winn in a formsuit, only this time intact and fully functioning, but still very much the suit of the High Controller integrated entity.

"This is our homeworld several centuries ago when the Centaurians were just beginning to fight their civil war in another part of the Galaxy. We had just taken our first few ventures out into the space beyond our world and the five moons," the High Controller explained.

Alanar was awestruck. Few had ever laid eyes on the Winn Winn origin planet and none from the Confederation side of the Galaxy. It was so huge and heavily developed that the underwater cities with their roots miles under the surface were visible from high orbit. The five moons displayed signs of extensive activity, too. They were thriving in the days when whole species were being conscripted to fight wars on behalf of the Centaurians.

"We believed we were alone and were content to think so. When they arrived we were near completely defenceless."

As if from nowhere, a fleet of strange vessels which Alanar could not recognise appeared, advancing on the Winn Winn homeworld. They fired missiles and primitive kinetic and energy weapons at the native ships and settlements. Time sped up and two of the moons turned to burning spheres, the others looked like battle-grounds as did the homeworld. All around floated the hulks of the ruined invasion force.

"We fought back with all we had and suffered horrific losses. But we won. And to most of us that was all that mattered. It was never to happen again."

Time jumped again to a now repaired homeworld and moons surrounded by a huge armada of thousands of ships: the mainstay war-spheres of the Winn Winn Empire.

"We united as never before and conquered the local space, finding those who had wronged us and reducing their own civilisation to the ashes of servitude. For hundreds of years we were supreme rulers of our dominion, determined never to burn again."

The view changed to that of a small force of swordships and shieldships facing war-spheres across a barren system.

"Until we met the Confederation. A power far greater than our own spanning thousands of worlds and claiming even more systems. You terrified us to our ancient cores and primal fears of the greater threat."

"We meant no harm," interjected Alanar. "The wounds of the Founder's War prevented us from taking any hostile action."

"Our Empire had become rigid, stagnant. Too set in its ways," explained the High Controller. "So we levelled all but a few of our forces against you in preparation for the war we felt you would undoubtedly bring."

"It left us vulnerable, though we did not realise it in our fear."

The view changed again to what looked like a small outpost with a single pair of war-spheres. They were joined briefly by what was eventually revealed to be a Tardig scout. It quickly vanished into stringspace.

"From random scouting missions it escalated to ship disappearances and then light skirmishes. When the assault came we couldn't have seen it nor had it happen at a worse time."

A full-blown space battle filled Alanar's mind.

"The Tardig War," he breathed as the images of shattered war-spheres and marauding Republic fleets continued and intensified. "We saw them as our saviours."

"They used our nature as an excuse to expand their influence. Once our fleet was destroyed, our worlds were blockaded and invaded. All the while they were forming ties with the Confederation."

"But they stabilised that area. There could've been an even greater war if they hadn't. Invading us completely undoes that!"

"We cannot argue over the subjective items of our war, Commodore," continued the High Controller, "but the aftermath is what led to the current crisis."

Multiple perspectives of worlds under blockade or invasion were shown. Stray war-spheres launched hit and run attacks, suicide bombers rushed troop formations and Winn Winn leaders ordered the fight to continue. In turn, the Tardigs launched their own attacks and crackdowns. Beings on both sides died in the thousands.

"Though the majority of our space forces and army lay in ruins, our leaders ordered the resistance to continue. We truly believed that the victory over the impossible of old could happen again if we just fought hard enough. But the Tardigs had gained too much ground."

A data-key was sent to Alanar's synth-sym.

"This will open the files given to you recently. It's a catalogue of what the Tardigs did to the Winn Winn to keep control of their new territory."

Using a side command, the Commodore applied the data-key and the files swarmed around them against a backdrop of sporadic firefights between the insurgency and Republic ships.

"What are those aerial files?"

"Relocation and holding centres," answered the High Controller. "What started as a divide, conquer and containment strategy has rapidly escalated to full-scale xenocide. The Winn Winn species no longer exists on worlds where it once flourished."

"And the attacks on uninhabited worlds?"

"The locations of centres where there were civil disturbances were reported initially, but the administration began using any event as a reason to sterilise them."

"What in the name of...?" he breathed. It was horrifying. "All those people..."

"Of the pre-war population of one hundred billion Winn Winn, less than thirty million can be confirmed alive at present and only those on the last remaining war-spheres are free."

"Those Winn Winn on Second Hygra...?"

"Are the last of the species that could be guaranteed their survival prior to the Republic launching its attack."

Such a scenario was terrifying and dark, but it left one critical question.

"But why move on the Confederation?"

"Many reasons. The power of the military began to far exceed that of both the civilian administration in the Republic and the former Empire and it became increasingly aggressive with the resistance actions and in trying to cover up the escalating deaths. They feared that if news got out, the Confederation would intervene and it would undermine their power. In one stroke they could take power in the Republic, wipe out the Winn Winn and launch a crippling blow to the Confederation to destroy its ability and will to fight."

"They couldn't possibly assume we'd intervene."

"History, Commodore," the entity said simply. "The Confederation was born out of the aftermath of the Centaurian Civil War. The death toll for some of the species involved was near catastrophic. Even Humanity suffered casualties in the billions. It took a century to recover and even then the Centaurian telekinetics *were* declared officially extinct. The Tardig military knew the Confederation would not allow another genocidal conflict to take place, accidental or not."

"We were on our way to alert the Navy when the Republic engaged us. And now the war has already begun."

The link ended and the real world pushed back into view.

"What can we do now, High Controller? Do you have battle plans, tactical information, anything that could help?"

"If the invasion has already begun there is little we can do to shift the strategic situation in your favour. We had hoped to pre-empt the Tardig deployments. Both Republic and resistance war scenarios predicted the loss of the entirety of the border edges of your Mid-Range by the most conservative estimates. This was in addition to the casualties amongst Confederation Navy and local defence forces, estimated at thirty percent destroyed, twenty percent moderately to severely-damaged and fifteen percent captured."

The Commodore considered the figures, comparing them to what he knew of area deployments. It was going to be a massacre, no matter what he did here. Second Hygra was just one of several dozen 'border' systems. Hundreds of millions of people were in the firing line.

"We would, however, like to make a request a request on the behalf of the Winn Winn resistance and species, Commodore."

He looked at the half-destroyed shell of a being before him. It had travelled so far and suffered so much, apparently only to deliver a pointless message and perhaps save a fraction of its species. This couldn't be an insurrection ploy. The invasion was real. He was convinced.

"By all means, High Controller."

"If I provide you with the communications protocols for our personnel on Second Hygra, will you contact them and organise an extraction? There may only be a few hundred of us left, but it is our only chance to survive as a species. They will recognise your command authority once it has been transferred from this body. They have been trained to disengage and plan guerrilla operations once the force against them becomes overwhelming."

A plan began taking shape within Alanar's mind as the information came together.

"I think, if we act very carefully," the Hygran began slowly, "we might not only be able to save your people but mine, too, and disrupt the invasion long enough to buy time for the rest of the Navy to act."

"Thank you, Commodore," said the dying Winn Winn. "We shall turn over all command data. If this body and unit do not survive the engagement, please inform our forces they have served their Empire well and should focus on recovering our species."

"I will. I have to speak with my officers. Rest as well as you can."

As he went through the door, the High Controller spoke again.

"And tell your High Admiral, Commodore, he was a worthy opponent."

Alanar shot the tank a confused look before carrying on. There was no time to analyse such obscure statements. He needed to find out the state of his forces. He located Roaragh and Morix29 in the mission planning office – the war room – holding a holo-conference with the other ships. In the few minutes it took him to get there, the outline was near fully formed. When he entered the room fell silent and he took the head of the table, a determined look on his face.

"Everyone, we have a new mission," he declared. "We're going back to Second Hygra. But before I go into detail, I need an update on our situation."

"Our swordships have all survived with no more than two hull breaches and the shieldships are all with us, but the *Pride of Kanassit* and the *Burning Plains* have suffered serious damage to their hull armour and engines," began Morix. "The rest have moderate upper armour damage. It's the Hygran craft and supports that have taken the real hits. The *Ambari* lost its lower decks to explosive missile hits and a third of its crew in the process. The light-cruiser *Shekto* is missing its forward PD guns and sensors.

"Both the destroyers *Leokst* and *Shatterfar* suffered only minor damage, but they were poorly crewed even before the operation began. The same is true of the defence cutters, except those two we lost and the *Hysix* which took several direct hits and barely functions now. It's preparing for evacuation as we speak. On average all ships lost eighty to ninety percent of their support in the attack."

She looked at him sceptically.

"Still want to try for the colony?"

The Captain stared as he thought, running through the calculations and points comprising his plan.

"Yes, but I need a few kinks in the plan ironed out first."

"Such as?" grunted Roaragh.

"A full sensor work up on the system and contact with our Marines, the colonial government and the Winn Winn troops. And a map of the mega-city," he datavised the Winn Winn protocols into the ship database.

"Why the Winn Winn?" asked the new captain incredulously. "They started this whole mess."

"They are now our new allies in this fight and their survival is connected to our own," explained Alanar. "And if we can't break through Republic jamming on our channels, we can use theirs to contact our forces."

A holographic schematic of the colony mega-city flickered over the table and was shortly followed by a real-time scaled image of the system.

"The system layout is patchy due to exit-entry point and electronic warfare interference," commented Morix, "and the mega-city map only shows visual survey data. It'll improve once contact is made. I'm efforting that now. Here's hoping our new friends are feeling co-operative."

Alanar nodded, looking back at the system hologram. The Republic had surrounded much of equatorial orbit and seemed to be using several points to run their forces through the system. Random patrols and planetary security groups were already beginning to be despatched. Standard operating procedure for any occupying force. And it was that which could help the operation.

"Alright, I know we're in a bad way right now," he began, "but maybe we can use that to our advantage. The enemy seems to think that we have fled the area or aren't worth bothering to search for seriously and are focusing on taking the colony – or most of it, anyway."

"The concentration of ships is in geo-synchronous orbit, over the mega-city specifically, and the equator in general to allow for easy access through the atmosphere now the OTR has been destroyed. The rest of the orbit and especially the poles are relatively unguarded."

The system map focused on the colony world at his datavised command.

"While our data is patchy, we will still be able to run two forces in through both poles and towards the city. They will consist of the capable smaller ships and support craft in the fleet, landing at multiple sites and evacuating as many key personnel as possible before boosting through the atmosphere and into clear space."

"Clear space?" cried one of the HDD captains. "There are hundreds of ships in orbit. We'll be massacred!"

"The *Ambari*, *Pride of Kanassit*, *Burning Plains* and *Shekto* will support the orbital insertions and flood the area with as much sensor clouding as possible," explained the Commodore. "Beforehand the remaining shieldships will deploy at maximum weapons range and engage the bulk of the enemy ship concentration, drawing them away."

He broadcast orders to the holographic projectors and the display zoomed out slightly. Images of the other four shieldships appeared and began firing at the enemy ships, drawing a small but rapidly increasing number of ships away. As the volume increased the polar attacks began and two translucent spheres appeared around them, representing the sensor disruption of the attackers.

"The attack on the poles will coincide with strikes across the system in the patrols by individual swordships to draw off further forces from orbit."

The system view zoomed out further to show the other worlds and patrol sites. A series of pulses highlighted half of the patrol formations.

"By targeting half of the patrols, we will force the enemy to commence general deployment to reinforce these groups and further weaken the orbiting forces."

The Republic formation over the planet diminished further.

"At this point the enemy ships will have fully deployed their own supports against our orbital attackers or the extraction forces just beginning their operation. They'll be fully exposed to the next phase of the plan."

The view focused on the engagement over Second Hygra. As the supports dispatched to the mega-city hit the atmosphere, an EP expelled a representation of an HDD defence cutter which promptly exploded amongst the mass of attackers; unleashing both a damaging blast and sensor frying radiation over the city.

"The damage should mirror that of a spatial implosion device and serve as a signal for our shieldship and polar attackers to disengage and our swordships to move in."

The shieldships disappeared and swordships entered the blast zone.

"They will cover the withdrawing evacuation forces until they are clear before jumping out to rejoin the rest of the fleet in open space and heading towards the shipyards in the Axiom system. They should be far enough outside of the combat zone to give us shelter."

He faded the holograms and looked at the assembled captains.

"I know this is asking a lot and the likelihood is we're going to lose even more people before this is over, but we have a duty to protect the Confederation and save as many Winn Winn as we can. What we do here today may well determine the course of the war."

The captains all began agreeing, one at a time.

"Alright. I'll evacuate the *Hysix* crew to the *Ambari* and dispatch engineers to prep it for its mission. All remaining supports will be assigned to the evacuation and polar-attack ships. I want everyone to prepare as best they can for deployment in one hour. Evacuation co-ordinates will follow shortly. Dismissed."

The holograms vanished, leaving him with Roaragh and Morix.

"I've made contact with the Winn Winn Ground Force Commander," she said. "They want to speak with you privately."

"Alright. Go and assist the fleet preparations. I'll call if I need help."

The pair nodded and left. The moment they left he opened the projectors to the waiting call of the Winn Winn Commander on Second Hygra who promptly appeared before him.

"Commodore Alanar," the formsuited figure addressed him. "I am Sub-Controller Lit'ko'ta'rek'th'Keela, assigned to the Winn Winn operation on your colony."

"Good to hear from you, Sub-Controller. I understand you wish to speak to me alone?"

"You claim to have authorisation from our High Controller to command this force? I demand proof. Where is the High Controller?"

"Receiving medical treatment for combat injuries, amongst other things. I'm afraid they are in a bad way right now."

The Sub-Controller made a low noise.

"How inconvenient for you. Nonetheless, I will not follow your orders without proof."

"Oh, in the name of – Listen, I have lost several ships and control of the space and much of the ground of the world which I was charged with defending. I can't retake it now, but I can at least save the people on it who might be able to do so later. I can't do that without your help."

The Sub-Controller remained stoic.

"And I owe your High Controller for at least giving me the information why this is happening to the Confederation. For all the animosity between our peoples I do not wish to see you enslaved or extinct."

That caught the Winn Winn's attention.

"You are aware of our predicament?"

"And what it means for our Galaxy, yes. Let me save your species, Sub-Controller, and as many of my people on the ground as possible. If we work together, perhaps we can knock the Republic off balance long enough for the Confederation to counter-attack and take back the system."

The link to the colony wobbled a little and the Sub-Controller briefly turned to someone off the projector range.

"It would seem we have little choice, Commodore, despite the dubious nature of your credentials," confessed the Winn Winn. "The Tardigs are commencing landings, despite the destruction of your orbital facilities."

"Damn," grunted Alanar. They were running out of time.

"If it is any consolation, the enemy lost at least ten ships when the demolition occurred."

Sadly, it wasn't, really. Alanar had hoped to delay the landings more than damage a statistically insignificant element of the invasion force. They would have more troops in the city now than he would have liked.

"Thank you, Sub-Controller. My second-in-command will handle the setting up of the evacuation planning and communications protocols. You have to act as quickly as possible when the operation begins. Once the Republic realises exactly what we are doing they will react to stop it if we do not move fast enough."

"And if and when they do," said the Sub-Controller, "I would prefer not to watch as my soldiers are incinerated by orbital guns."

"We won't let it get that far," promised the Hygran earnestly. "Even if I have to send this ship into the invasion fleet, the evacuation force will get through."

"I hope you do not have to keep that promise, Commodore. For I have seen better soldiers betray similar bonds in better situations."

Alanar nodded.

"I understand, Sub-Controller. I'll hand over now. Good luck!"

The image faded away as it was linked to Morix29. He sat in the silence and loneliness of the mission planning room. Disengaged from the situation, it was all so hard to grasp. The Republic, one of the Confederation's closest allies, was not only butchering an entire species, it was apparently launching an invasion the likes of which the Galaxy had never witnessed in thousands of years at least. Even compared to the Winn Winn or Founder's Wars, this was spectacular and terrifying. And his fleet was right in the middle of it. Any future beyond today seemed so distant and uncertain.

It was a disorientating feeling. The deck his chair rested on seemed to tilt with the weight of consideration. How many had died already, he wondered, reviewing the limited data he had of the area the High Controller had described. There weren't many 'major' worlds like Second Hygra, but there were several dozen colonies owned by both the Confederation or its member worlds; interstellar trade posts and military or police bases of a similar number and then there were the incalculable numbers of vessels on the shipping lanes and unregistered settlements and drifts.

The Confederation and its members did not keep track of settlement and travel to a huge extent, unless it disrupted military security or caused a major issue. From where Alanar was sitting, it could well be the casualties would be in the millions for they were already certainly in the hundreds of thousands. Morix appeared before him in tiny form, sitting on the edge of the main table.

"I have identified key evacuation sites for all ground forces on Second Hygra to head for once the attack begins."

"And the transfer of the troops and material between ships?"

"Underway. We should be at full readiness in ten minutes. My avatar is installed on the Hysix. Lucky for us we had a freshly-damaged defence cutter to play with."

Alanar sighed.

"We'll be lucky if our plan to use it as a bomb works. We both know there's only a sixty-five percent chance it will work."

"Better than a regular spatial implosion device. What if it fails?"

"I'll order our ship and two of the attacking shieldships inwards to the colony to cover the city. The polar attackers will join the remaining shieldships. It's not a perfect solution but it is the best I have."

She was quiet.

"You have something on your mind," he stated simply.

"Have you considered what this means?"

"The defence of the colony?"

"No, the retreat from the colony. For the Hygran species."

The truth was, Alanar had been ignoring the implications of Second Hygra's loss since he had decided to evacuate his forces and withdraw.

"Yes. No matter how many people we save today, we'll still lose Hygra's only hope for a homeworld and a major asset outside of the home system. And I'll be the one who lost it."

"It's one way to get into history," the UIPE said wryly. "Better than dying in a pointless defence. Ever wonder if we'd be better off had the Centaurian Empire stuck around?"

"We'd have more guns, but we'd still be fighting this war," he responded quickly.

"So, it's a war now?"

The Commodore spread his arms.

"A Republican military force has attacked us and is invading our territory, and I have intelligence that indicates something similar is happening elsewhere. I'd call that a war."

"There has been no declaration, though. It could still be a rogue operation."

"Oh, wake up, Morix!" the Commodore yelled, slamming two fists down on the table and standing over her tiny form. "Our colony is in ruins and we've lost ships in an unprovoked attack by forces acting in accordance with Tardig Republic military doctrine of announcing intent and demanding one of two responses: fight or surrender. They stated they were acting on behalf of the Republic. Does that sound like a rogue force to you? Does it?!"

Rather than look taken aback, Morix grew to a more proportionate size, keeping her expression neutral.

"Commodore, by Navy authority I am obligated to obey your orders and I appreciate the stress of your position," she said placidly, "but do not speak to me in that way if you wish to be thought well of by your forces."

Rather than argue, Alanar collapsed back into a chair, exhausted.

"I'm sorry, Morix. The situation is getting to me. Our lives all hang in the balance and I still have to consider those we are abandoning on Second Hygra to the invasion forces."

The UIPE was looking right at him, a furious expression quickly spreading across her visage and catching the Commodore by the same surprise he had felt upon seeing her back on the colony when the subversion of her partitions become apparent.

"Apology accepted, Alanar," she began, "but I fear you may be correct in what you were saying. However, for such an invasion to be so successful in its opening moves against Second Hygra the assigned forces would need to know several key pieces of information."

"Such as?"

"They'd need the locations and patrol vectors of our ships to know when the supports and Marines were deployed or deploying and at their most vulnerable and our communications protocols."

"Something only fleet captains would have access to," he breathed.

"And I think I've found the traitorous scum who let the Republic into the system," announced the UIPE. "She's broadcasting wideband to our ground forces now."

A hologram appeared between the two of them, representing a familiar figure.

"Attention all Confederation and Hygran forces on Second Hygra," Navat proclaimed to the entire system. "I am Hygran Defence Directorate Ship-Commander Navat aboard the light-cruiser *Shamsha*. The Confederation and Hygran ships in orbit have been driven out of the system by forces from the Tardig Republic which are now landing on the surface of your colony in the thousands.

"Despite the attempts to stave off the landing forces, they will completely occupy the surface in under two hours. Further resistance will only continue to damage the mega-city and cost more lives in a meaningless sacrifice.

"You may believe others will come for you. They will not. Other systems have already fallen to the Republic advance and all possible responders have been engaged and suppressed. Therefore, I appeal to all resisting forces on Second Hygra to surrender to the Republic occupation forces. Those who do will be held on Republic worlds until the end of the present conflict and treated well. Those who do not will be liquidated. Make the right choice; for Second Hygra, your families and yourselves."

The transmission terminated.

"Where is that fu– "

"The *Shamha* is in high orbit around Second Hygra, escorting a fresh wave of transports towards the colony. They appear to be preparing to hit an environmental station on the far side of the planet."

"I see," said Alanar, more calmly now and calling up an image of the system in his synth-sym. "Make that convoy the first of our targets when we begin the raids."

Morix smirked.

"Very good, Commodore."

"Driven out of the system, my ass," he muttered, standing up again. "Let's get the show on the road."

Morix nodded.

"See you in the C3C."

He marched out of the room towards the nerve centre of the swordship, revitalised by the burning need to destroy the traitorous Navat – better yet, destroy the *Shamsha* or cripple it and arrest her. A humiliating trial and prison term was exactly what she deserved.

But as quickly as that thought occurred, he banished it, using his synth-sym to focus on and run through combat routines. An emotional outburst in the privacy of the mission planning room was one thing, but it had no place in battle. When he arrived the crew looked as ready as they would ever be.

"All ships report ready to execute mission objectives," reported Morix.

Alanar stood next to the command podium, not taking his eyes off the tactical displays of the fleet, now in position to attack. He took a deep breath, silently willing his plan to succeed.

"Order the shieldships to begin the orbital strike," he began, "and cycle up the drives on the swordships. Insertion forces will depart five minutes after we do."

"Issuing orders now," came the reply from the Communications Officer.

One by one, the attacking shieldships began entering stringspace to hit the fleet orbiting Second Hygra. Now they would have to wait and hope that they could maintain communications or timing and educated guesswork would become the key to running this operation.

The minute of silent anticipation was torture and time appeared to slow throughout the system. Eventually, though, it had to be broken.

"I have been contacted by the *Deadly Vanguard*," Communications half-shouted in jubilation. "The attack has begun and the enemy is responding."

The Commodore allowed himself a small smile as the displays updated.

"*Melee Method* is cleared to depart and engage," he ordered.

"Yes, Commodore."

Melee Method disappeared into stringspace. Alanar reviewed its target list; essentially half of the Republic's transit points across the system. One after the other, the swordship would attack the points, disrupting military support operations and drawing security away from the colony. *Star*

Dragon's task set was essentially the same. The *Vigilant* was to hit existing forces trying to secure the system and the colony. The Republic would have no choice but to disperse at least some of its forces.

"Contact established with *Melee Method*! Engagement with light security forces in progress. Orbital attack force is under increasing enemy fire but reports other ships jumping out."

"*Star Dragon* is clear to engage in operations against targets."

"Issuing orders."

Another entry point opened before a ship of the fleet and the assault continued. Displays switched and split to cover the situations over Second Hygra and with the swordships. As the battles unfolded, Alanar prepared himself to enter the fight.

"*Star Dragon* has engaged the enemy. Looks like it's caught an exiting convoy completely by surprise."

The relevant display expanded to show the *Star Dragon* destroying three Republic attack frigates and crippling two more.

"Alright, prepare to deploy to our first target," the Commodore said calmly, his pulse quickening. "Are our insertion forces and their cover ready?"

"Yes, Commodore," replied Morix. "My avatar on the Hysix is also ready."

"Commence our deployment and order the insertion forces to begin their countdown as soon as we make contact. If it does not occur within three minutes, then go ahead anyway."

"Sending orders.

"Jump plotted. Space-lane interface is go."

"Insertion and support forces have sent conformation."

"Commence jump!"

The *Vigilant Watchman* slid into stringspace and began hurtling toward its targets, severing its communications with the rest of its forces. Soon they would begin the key part of the operation and it was up to the swordships to draw as much of the invasion force off as possible.

"Exiting stringspace!"

The exit point opened directly inside the convoy led by the *Shamsha* in order to give the enemy as little time as possible to respond and fragment them. It appeared to work.

"Obtaining targeting information...thirty-six targets identified."

"Weapons lock on ten close-ships."

"Detecting active locks from six – seven – nine craft."

"All weapons fire at will!"

The weapons banks of beam lasers, missiles and kinetic bullet launchers rotated and angled to unleash their payloads on the assigned targets. In moments holes were blown in armour and hulls had several chunks lopped off. The transports were not well armed, being built mainly for landings and point defence for intercepting missiles and fighters.

Shamsha, on the other hand, despite its size, was a warship and armed with weapons befitting that title. Seconds after the opening salvo it retaliated. A detonation thrummed through the ship. Immediately, Alanar knew the damage would be worse where the ship had been hit.

"Multiple missile strikes on the damaged sections of the forward hull," came the report. "Other hits from PD weapons elsewhere have been ineffectual."

"Can you locate the *Shamsha*?" asked Alanar. "And get me that communications uplink!"

The pauses from Morix, the Sensor Officer and Communications Officer were unsettling and told him everything before he heard it.

"The *Shamsha* is using some kind of IFF scattering technology to conceal its location."

"We are unable to uplink right now because of jamming from one of the ships in this force."

"Continue free firing until we clear the area," ordered the Commodore. "Let me know as soon as we can jump safely."

"Detecting multiple exit points!"

"Prioritise those EPs. Numbers and data?"

"Confirmed, twenty EPs. Looks like strike-cruisers."

How could they have responded so quickly, wondered Alanar for a brief moment before he came to the realisation. Navat's broadcast, of course! She had lured them here. And he had fallen for it.

"Take those cruisers down asap!" he demanded.

"Commodore," Morix warned, "those transports are closing on our position. Fast!"

He looked at the display. What were they up to?

"Use our KBLs to take them out, but our focus needs to be on those cruisers," he ordered, looking to Roaragh and Morix. "Any ideas?"

"Could be trying to swamp us," the Acting Captain guessed. "Suicidal, though."

Morix was quiet at first, but then became urgent in her tone.

"We need to activate the entire internal defences now!" she said vigorously. "Lock down every section immediately and get heavy weapons to the crew."

"You think they're going to board us?" asked Alanar incredulously.

"This is one of the command craft for the fleet. It makes sense."

"Issue orders to the crew and prepare for counter-boarding ops," ordered Alanar. "I want as many of those transports taken out as possible. Evasive action!"

The *Vigilant* began to manoeuvre out of the convoy formation slowly but surely with the transports closing in all the time. Inside the ship, section shut-off partitions began moving into place, sealing off individual parts from each other. While this was underway, crew members began breaking open auxiliary weapons containers, automated KSR batteries lowered into position and armed battle robots began activating and taking up positions.

"If they board, what are we looking at?" Alanar asked Morix.

"With the bulk of Marines on Second Hygra we are particularly vulnerable. The robots and KSR (auto) were intended as supports, not a standalone force," confessed the UIPE. "The crew all have varying levels of combat experience and are being advised to cluster where they can."

"So, if they board?"

"We'd lose the sections in the immediate vicinity of landing sites and any that have minimal personnel or defences adjoining them. Key strategic sections off the ship should be fine. Everything else…we'll have to see. The Republic troops come in many varieties and qualities."

"As soon as they hit I want a section of the display dedicated to our ship status. And get me a countdown on the jump drives. We need to get out of here."

Another detonation rocked the ship.

"More ships jumping in. Looks like battlecruisers."

"SLIDE will be at full readiness in four minutes."

"Initial impacts expected in two minutes."

"Can we fast-jump?" asked Roaragh.

"With all these breaches and weapons fire, I wouldn't recommend it. We could rip off the forward hull," said Alanar. "Looks like we'll have to prepare for our guests."

He walked over to the C3C weapons locker and began handing out weaponry, selecting a kinetic slam rifle for himself.

"We can also slow them down a little by venting the relevant sections," advised Morix.

"That will slow our response too," said the large Kin-Sai.

"Save it for a last resort," decided Alanar. "We might need to have the freedom to move. And they'll have armour."

He activated the rifle's acceleration arrays that would fire hyper-velocity rounds into the selected targets, setting the rounds themselves to explode on impact. The concussive force of the blasts would inflict enough damage to hinder enemy movement by inducing physical harm and casualties to be cleared. It was easier to walk over corpses than screaming wounded.

Where to shoot, though, he wondered, racking his brains for any relevant combat techniques. The Confederation Navy generally identified the limbs as prime targets and made other such highly-generalised recommendations. Specific species profiling was considered impolitic and highly-concerning to member races. How he cursed such ideas now.

"Impact in ten seconds."

"Location?"

"Upper hull. Close to dome two. We don't have anything in that area. Other predicted areas are on our starboard side hull and the rest of the upper sectors, occurring within the next thirty seconds."

"Five seconds!"

"Prepare for impact."

Alanar turned to Roaragh.

"Can I count on you to continue this operation if I engage the enemy?"

The Kin-Sai frowned.

"Commodore, you cannot risk yourself –"he began.

"I can if they threaten key sectors."

"Impact!"

A dull rumble was audible briefly as, elsewhere, the first of several transports crashed through the hull and began unleashing boarding forces. New tactical updates appeared on the displays.

"Report?"

"Damage to hull armour and decompression in all surrounding sections. We've lost monitoring coverage in the impact zone."

"Another two transports down, but support is continuing to arrive."

"Alright, focus all fire on the strike-cruisers. Their heavy hitters won't risk harming the transports from that range."

It would mean more Republic troops onboard, but they could hopefully manage them.

"Detecting movement in the first impact area. Looks like they are opening their main bays to deploy forces. It's tearing open new breaches."

"Four more transports just breached," came the word after more rumblings.

Still too far from the key zones and personnel concentrations. That could let them amass a sizeable force. Alanar ground his teeth.

"How many left?" he asked Morix.

"Seven more before we can jump," she replied. "So, if it's infantry, we could be looking at thousands of troops. And that is the best case. If they deploy support vehicles we could sustain huge damage. The Marines had most of the heavy weapons."

He refocused on the Acting Captain.

"Can I count on you?"

"Naturally, Commodore."

The Hygran nodded graciously, feeling the weight of the rifle slung on his back. He'd never killed anyone before. Not many people in the Confederation Navy or the Second Hygra system had. How many had felt a similar weight on their shoulders?

"Impacts continuing. Enemy support is restricting fire to isolated areas."

"Enemy sighted on board! Repeat! We have enemies sighted. Looks like troopers moving in standard boarding patterns."

The display showed bulky, armour-clad figures moving through the corridors and taking up positions in them. No battles yet. But only for now. If this happened on the other ships, then the prospects of safely rescuing those on the colony would be difficult.

"SLIDE has been cycled."

"Jump to the next target," ordered Alanar.

"Jumping."

Up next on the list was a small patrol group. They could wipe it out and deal with the boarders before the jump inwards towards the colony. As the *Vigilant Watchman* began its transit, the stress exerted in the damage exposed sections of the ship and its invading companions.

Two transports were torn away and destroyed by the tidal forces, and breaches widened and worsened, shaking the swordship violently. Seconds later, the transit was completed and the burning, damaged remnants of the Republic convoy and its supports were left to recover. In short order, the swordship re-entered normal space and encountered the three patrolling attack frigates.

"Transit complete."

"Achieving target lock."

"Prepare full missile barrage."

"Lock achieved."

"Fire!"

Three fireballs quickly filled a display section, rapidly dissipating into space. Now to deal with the boarders.

"Are the transports transmitting any signals?" Alanar demanded.

"Not that we can detect. Jamming is at full coverage."

"Good. Show me the ship."

The displays showed a schematic of the *Vigilant*, its impact and damage zones, and the positions of all personnel aboard. The enemy had established nine separate staging areas all over the ship, mostly on the upper starboard. As they expanded they would consolidate and co-ordinate, eventually hitting the main central areas.

And so the problem became apparent: defend and risk losing the ship to an increasingly co-ordinated enemy, or attack and risk that happening faster? He needed to delay.

"Are there any robots capable of making fast attacks and recons?" the troubled Commodore asked.

"Not on this class of ship, no," replied Roaragh. "Recon is best suited to the closest Marine squads."

"Issue orders to all Marines to organise hit and run ops where they can. And try to contact the rest of the fleet. Find out what's going on."

"We can't stay here for long, Commodore," warned Roaragh. "They'll notice a missing patrol eventually and if the boarders take our batteries we'll be in trouble."

The thought of turrets cutting apart the ship made him shudder internally. A quiet alert sounded, signalling the beginning of an engagement. It was between enemy troops and one of the internal defence cannons. It lasted less than twenty seconds, resulting in the destruction of the cannon and no enemy casualties. Another alert. And another. And another. All over the ship fighting began between the first line of automated defences.

"How is this happening so quickly?" he wondered aloud.

"The automated internal defences are not designed to operate under these conditions," the Acting Captain answered. "Nothing was."

"How are the ship-board weapons holding up?" Alanar asked.

"We have most of them, but the missile batteries are running low on ammunition and the kinetic ammunition is at fifty percent."

"That went down awfully quickly!"

"We were given the inventory deemed appropriate for the mission we were originally given," explained Morix. "All the ships have minimal armament and are Age of Foundation class."

"So, we're pretty much the worst possible force configuration for facing an invasion?"

"No! Can you imagine how disastrous this would have been had just the defence cutters been here?" the UIPE pointed out. "Anyway, the point is we can hold our own against a standard attack force for a while, as long as we deal with these boarders."

Alanar nodded slowly, revising his plan in his head.

"We stage our clear-out operation here, shooting down any ships that come to investigate. We can take out the staging areas one at a time. It'll let us focus our forces."

"Very good," said Morix. "The best choice is probably here."

A breached section of the ship lit up.

"It's closest to our major concentration and quite small," the UIPE explained.

"Alright, co-ordinate our assault with the ship's defences and keep me advised," Alanar ordered. "In the meantime I need a way of assessing the status of the rest of the operation. Suggestions?"

Morix flared away and the Communications Officer stood.

"If the troops can seize an enemy vessel we might be able to re-establish contact through their communications."

"I'll make it top priority once we clear that first area."

"Until then we can try to establish visual contact," added Roaragh.

"We should be able to tell when the *Hysix* self-destructs."

The Commodore hoped they could clear the ship before that happened. He didn't like the idea of Tardigs being onboard when the evacuation began. Especially if they took or attacked the launch-landing bays. Looking up at the screens it was clear the first assault was about to begin. Several screens showed marines sneak up on Tardig soldiers and silently kill or disable them. That couldn't last for long, though.

No sooner had the thought formed in his mind than a series of gun battles erupted before him as the Tardigs became aware of what was happening all around them and began trying to signal each other.

He could almost feel the various blasts and projectiles thrumming through the air. A charge blew a hole in one of the bulkheads, collapsing the ceiling of a corridor and shorting out the onboard sensors.

Elsewhere the Confederation Navy forces began encountering increasingly fierce resistance all over the ship. There were too many of them and they were far too prepared. Perhaps it was time to consider a new plan. He would give them a little more time.

"We have three squads approaching, through ventilation ducts and access tubes, one of them enemy ships. They don't seem to have guarded those properly," advised Morix over the loudspeakers. "Once they gain access, the vessel's networks should be infiltrated by one of my programmes."

Let's hope so, thought Alanar, as another breach was reported, or there won't be enough of a ship left to make a difference.

The battle slowly began taking shape along more coherent lines as both sides took up strong points and reinforcements arrived. Navy forces didn't seem to be retreating, but they were not advancing either. The same was true of the Tardigs. Clear zones of control were now emerging instead of the progressive assault they had planned.
Dammit!

The uplinks showed the stealth squads. They quietly exited their hiding places and began trying to locate an entrance into the ship. The area around it was a ruin. Crew quarters, engineering rooms, gymnasia – it was all lying or floating in half-destroyed ashes from the impact.

A massive detonation suddenly jolted and rocked the deck below their feet.

"What the fuck was that?!" demanded Alanar.

"I released the stabilisation and protection controls for Dome Two," explained Morix. "Over five hundred Tardigs just got blown into space and a gap has opened up for us to exploit."

She materialised in front of the command podium, puzzled at the Commodore's irritated expression.

"They were using it as a staging and control area. I had to do something," she explained.

"Next time, could you please let me know before you start blowing off parts of the ship?" asked Alanar in an exasperated tone.

"Of course. In the meantime, though, we can take advantage of the chaos I've created in their forces."

The Marines pushed forward and into several places of the Tardig areas, but no significant progress was being made. No-one had said it out loud but the goals had clearly changed: they had to gain access to that boarding craft.
Outside the embattled swordship, two Tardig craft entered normal space.

"Reading two Tardig attack frigates on patrol," reported the sensor analysis officer. "They are targeting us!"

"Use our beam weapons to take them out," ordered Alanar. They would need the more explosive weapons to engage the enemy over the colony.

The attack frigates were under no such restrictions and opened fire with everything they had. Too much for all the beam weaponry to deal with.

Explosions were reported in all main sections of the ship with thrumming and rocking to confirm it. Then the weapons lock from the *Vigilant's* guns was confirmed and the Confederation ship opened fire. Within seconds one ship was destroyed, the other heavily damaged.

"We lost several vital weapons and sensor arrays in that attack, Commodore," said Roaragh, "and there is no guarantee that the enemy doesn't know our location. We cannot wait any longer."

"We need those communications, Acting Captain, and the starting gun has not been fired yet."

"If they send a larger force our way and surround us –"

"I am well aware of what will happen!" interrupted Alanar harshly. "Now, stand to and await my orders."

The battle was going badly enough outside without one breaking out in the C3C.

"Our troops have gained access to the transport's networks," said Morix, closing her eyes while she uploaded the virus. "We should know what is going on shortly."

The battle for the *Vigilant's* interior raged away in the swordship's corridors and compartments. The Tardigs were falling back everywhere now, trying to regroup from Morix's manoeuvre and those of the Marines and armed crew. It was far from a victory, though. With any luck they could purge the ship once they reached safe ground.

"And…got it!" declared Morix victoriously. "Connecting enemy communications to our own now."

"Very good. Order our unengaged units to secure choke-points and set up kill zones around key areas of the ship," ordered Alanar. "Then start filtering our forces into them. The bots and Morix can fight delaying actions until we can get them purged outside of the combat zone."

The displays slowly began changing as the Navy troops began to fall back. If the enemy could be kept out of the areas essential to the new mission they essentially had this won if they could survive the gauntlet over the colony.
Alanar looked at Morix, her computer-generated face giving away no emotion.

"Morix," he probed, quietly walking up to her. "Report please?"

"It looks as though the plan is going accordingly," she said. "Our ground attack and evacuation is progressing well and the enemy is devoting increasing resources to locate and destroy our space elements."

"I'm sensing a 'but' coming, though."

"You'd be right. The enemy engaged the *Burning Plains* and the *Pride of Kanassit*. The projected outcome is not good, frankly."

The loss of the shieldships would cost them dearly. All hope of success lay in the next stage of the plan.

"Wait!" she said suddenly. "I'm getting something. Unidentified EP opening over the colony!"

"This is it!" shouted Alanar. "Prepare to jump to Second Hygra"

"They are still analysing what it is," continued Morix. "They think it's a battlecruiser based on power output – idiots! Jump protocols initiated. Countdown T-minus one minute."

"Can we broadcast to the other ships?" asked Alanar.

"Not yet, but they are aware," the UIPE replied before opening her eyes to stare in revelation. "Detonation!"

The blast could be seen throughout the system as the *Hysix's* onboard computer initiated a chain reaction while it was still partially connected to stringspace. Those on ships nearby in orbit wouldn't see it as the empty space around them collapsed into a surging energy and gravity maelstrom. Anyone with unprotected eyes on the surface would scream in pain as they dissolved before the unrelenting light. All across the planet and in orbit sensors failed, structures buckled and communications died.

Even in space, vessels were not safe. Stringspace ripples shook craft into normal space, the smaller ones either badly damaged or torn to shreds outright. All Republic activity in the system was disrupted to some extent, just as the Confederation began the final leg of its operation.

As the last ten seconds counted away, Alanar felt a renewed confidence in what they were doing. They could rescue the Winn Winn survivors and those others on the colony. It would still take a real effort but they could do it.

"Jumping."

The *Vigilant* leapt into stringspace as the last of the ripples ceased, along with the other swordships. In seconds they would be among the Tardigs in orbit, with their most powerful weapons primed. The Republic was going to be given a battering it wouldn't soon forget. When they emerged they reacted immediately.

"Achieving weapons lock in fire."

"Identifying targets."

"Opening L-L bay doors, preparing to receive evacuation groups."

"Charging weapons and opening energy stores."

"Basic level security established. Commencing ship-side troop disengagement."

"Morix, see what you can do using the ship-side equipment to take out those Tardigs."

"Can you get engineering to do it, please?" she asked "I'm busy with communications."

Unwilling to argue, Alanar nodded at Roaragh who began contacting engineering.

"All weapons fire at will," he added loudly.

Not three seconds later a beam of energy smashed through a battlecruiser's armour, the opening salvo of a stream of fire directed against the Tardig fleet which, as predicted, had almost all their weapons facing the wrong way. Space was already filled with an unimaginable field of dead or dying ships – or at least the space where the Tardig fleet was concentrated. All the Navy had to do was add to it.

"Communication uplink complete," reported Morix. "Evacuation orders sent and connections with other ships are go."

"Excellent! Let me know when evacuation is complete and we'll get out of here."

The smaller craft on Second Hygra began rocketing to the space above from their evacuation points once they were full. Communications were positive. A lot of Winn Winn had been saved along with many marines and key colonial government members. They might not save the colony but they could get out the people central to retaking it in future.

"Enemy fire is minimal, Commodore," the SAO reported. "They still seem to be in shock and that wreckage field is only making things easier."

"Alright, ease up on the weapons fire and pick your shots. Let's not be over-confident, though. Doesn't mean we are out of the woods yet."

"Estimated time to evacuation completion is approximately ten minutes," noted Morix.

There was the familiar distant rumble as the enemy began to return fire more substantially. Their missiles and KB rounds would soon turn into an endless rain. The Navy contingent could not remain here long. Alanar personally doubted that they could even stay the whole ten minutes. They might have to make do with the rescue of only most of the ships and their personnel. It would still be a positive result, but –

A huge blast directly beneath the C3C knocked everyone around violently.

"The enemy is using ground-based weapons to target us and the evacuation force!"

"Switch fifty percent of PD fire to the surface and begin minor evasive manoeuvres," ordered Alanar.

"That's not all," warned Morix. "Those boarders are launching an attack on the L-L bay, main engineering and I suspect one aimed at here. They are getting desperate."

"How are we holding up?" asked the Commodore.

"Uncertain. They have –" she almost laughed. "They have several armoured support units in play! They must have just got them online."

"They are desperate," Alanar said quietly before speaking up. "Alright, continue monitoring the fighting and let me know if we need to head down there."

Republican Guard ships continued to snipe from the debris, more and more of them turning into the fight, recovering from the blast.

"Picking up enemy support and strike craft inbound from the orbital fleet. Over six hundred in the first wave!" warned the SAO.

"Shit! Launch all ordnance at them in burst and PD mode. Do not let them through!" Alanar ordered.

It would not be enough to fend them off entirely, but what else could they do? Missiles, shells and beams thundered out towards the mass of smaller ships, fragments, shockwaves and energised particles eroding, damaging and shredding their hulls.

The tiny craft began blossoming into fireballs or breaking apart under the barrage, those who survived returning fire with smaller armaments that individually would do little damage, but could collectively cripple sections of ships.

"The first evacuees are boarding now via emergency landing procedures. Medical teams are responding."

"The main medical area is coming under attack from boarding parties. Personnel and wounded are evacuating and marines are failing back."

"Engage plan Gladio," ordered Alanar. "Leave nothing for them to use. How is that ship-side counter-measure set coming?"

"Engineering is getting ready to blow the other two domes once they are over-run and they have several radiation and depressurisation tactics ready to go."

"Use them where possible without harming our people. I don't want those armoured supports in my command centre!" the Hygran commanded.

The smaller enemy ships attacking the trio of swordships made their first pass, picking out exposed areas and equipment, and tearing into them before hurtling past. Only a small minority had survived the initial assault. But they were only a tiny part of the true force the enemy could bring to bear once they recovered. They had to speed this up.

"Anyway we can pick up the pace?" he asked no-one in particular.

"We could descend further into the atmosphere," suggested the Communications Officer after a pause punctuated with weapons fire.

"We would be more vulnerable but landing time would shorten."

Alanar looked at Morix, then Roaragh.

"Well, we're already between a hostile fleet and a hostile planet," said Alanar. "It doesn't get more vulnerable than that. Take us in closer and signal the other ships."

The swordships began sinking into the atmosphere slowly but surely. As the flight paths shortened for the evacuation craft so too did the distance enemy fire had to travel from the surface batteries of the Republican Guards, which became obvious moments into the descent.

A missile slammed into the top of the swordship's hull, blowing it apart and sending shockwaves throughout the ship.

"Gravity is beginning to interact with the hull," explained Morix. "As we descend the effects on the ship will worsen."

"Can't we compensate with the SI field?" asked Alanar.

"The SI field is out of commission where the hull has been pierced or blown apart by boarders. Speaking of which—"

There was a horrific screeching sound as a Tardig ship lodged at a downward angle in the hull was torn out under the pull of the new sources of gravity, plummeting towards the surface.

The C3C watched it happen on the screens in silence.

Alanar had an idea.

"Continue descent and begin a lateral role, full three and sixty," he ordered. "Let's see if we can shake off these parasites."

Slowly the ship began to roll, the groans and shrieks of badly-damaged hull sections swiftly following.

"Rotate weapons array to maintain coverage," Alanar said firmly.

The floor tilted slightly as the SI AG projectors came under increasing strain.

"Can we increase projector strength?" he asked Morix.

"Only for three minutes. We have to complete the roll in that time!"

A missile smashed into the tail section.

"Do it. And let's see if we can't speed up the turn."

The tide of gravity was stemmed and the *Vigilant* flipped fully upside down, more and more of the enemy transports falling away or breaking in two.

The turn completed as the AG boost failed and the damage reports flooded in.

"AG blow-outs in sections A-87 and A-85."

"Hull breaches on all decks, sealing now."

"Casualties on all decks, medical staff are overstretched."

"Alanar," said Morix, "there are only two transports left attached and the enemy is in disarray, but we lost half our AG net."

"Crap! At least there is an upside, though. And the evacuation?"

"We'll be done in three minutes."

"Enemy ships are clearing the wreckage and blast zone!"

"How many?"

"Fifty plus, with support craft accompanying. And ground fire is increasing!"

"Shit," swore Alanar quietly. "Let's hope our little manoeuvre does the trick."

And then there was the small matter of jumping out of the area. Atmospheric jumps were complicated.

The three swordships on a dedicated section of one of the display screens did not look in good shape. *Star Dragon* had breaches all along its forward section from what looked like numerous ramming attempts. *Melee Method's* main propulsion array had been badly damaged and a deep breach had been gouged in its central sections, perhaps from an explosion or collision. He wondered what condition the other ships would be in.

"Ship-side reports indicate no more attacks by boarders."

"Send out some squads to keep them off balance."

A dozen missiles smashed into the upper hull armour and disintegrated a large chunk of it, shockwaves disabling several localised systems.

"Are we able to punch out of this?" Alanar asked Roaragh.

"Possibly," the Kin-Sai said, checking over his data. "If we can get high enough we might be able to avoid engaging that fleet directly and a close range.

"Let's try that option first."

Two KB rounds struck the lower hull, their impacts reverberating around the blast zones and into the ship, injuring the crew in their dozens.

"Energy transfer lines to the starboard engine array have been ruptured. Sealing now. Manoeuvring is down by thirty percent."

The countdown timer in his head continued to tick back and his synth-sym monitored the evacuation. They could do this!

"Enemy ships are locking on. Missile flow increasing exponentially."

Even if the ship was horrendously damaged.

The timer reached one minute.

"Alright, take us to the edge of the atmosphere and prepare to jump out," Alanar decided. "All weapons aim towards that fleet. We have to get out of here."

"All of our evacuation craft should make it aboard by then, bar one, Commodore," warned Morix.

The Hygran swore and sighed heavily. There was always one.

"Which ship?"

"The destroyer *Shatterfar* has evacuated a large Winn Winn force, but it's suffering engine difficulties. It needs another two minutes."

Crunch time.

Do they have SLIDEs still?"

"Yes, but they cannot execute an atmo-jump until they reach this height. They will need support."

The options were few. A brief review of the weaponry of the landed evacuation ships showed they were ill-equipped to provide cover. One of the larger ships would have to go back.

"Which one of our swordships is best placed to survive going back for them?" he asked the SAO.

"Probably the *Star Dragon*, but it'll be a close run thing."

Alanar turned to the Communications Officer.

"Signal *Star Dragon* to pick up the *Shatterfar*," he ordered.

Another detonation shook the deck. In a nearby hallway, a support collapsed.

"*Star Dragon* signals it will not go back," the Communications Officer reported incredulously. "Their Acting Captain says they will not go on a suicide mission."

There was no time to argue.

"Take us back down there," decided Alanar. "Full speed! We can scoop up the destroyer and use our inertia to slingshot us away out the other side of the planet."

"Commodore, that's –" Morix tried to protest.

"Do as I say, dammit! I will not lose those people."

There was a brief pause and then the crew went to work. *The Vigilant Watchman* began to rapidly turn and descend back towards the planet.

"Clear that launch-landing bay and prepare for impact damage. Guide that destroyer in as best we can," the Hygran yelled, analysing instruments on the command podium and maintaining a constant data-stream with the pilots. "I want minimal casualties."

The Navy ship continued to dive down towards the colony, dodging the majority of the fire being sent its way. Those shots that did make their mark were particularly damaging. As gravity began to naturally increase again it, too, made its mark on the hull. Plating already pried open was sheared off, breaches worsened and gravatic fluctuation threw crewmen around. The transit would be even worse when the ascent recommenced, Alanar imagined.

"Contact with the destroyer in twenty seconds," reported Morix.

"Preparing to initiate rapid acceleration and ascent for slingshot."

"All hands prepare for rapid planetside manoeuvring," announced Roaragh over the loudspeakers.

On the sensor analysis section of the display screen, the other two swordships were shown jumping away before the descending enemy fleet could reach them. They quickly changed targets, though, plotting new intercept courses to take on the *Vigilant*. And those support craft crept ever closer, despite the PD fire.

"Five seconds!" hollered Morix.

"This is going to be tight," declared Alanar through clenched teeth.

The swordship decelerated and began pulling up, literally scooping the much smaller destroyer into its L-L bay. The tiny ship travelling at that speed was too much for the cushioning AG fields to withstand now they were so badly weakened. It smashed into and through one of the bay racks, collapsing several more in the process before finally coming to rest.

"We have them!"

"Good! Now let's get out of here. Full acceleration!" ordered Alanar.

Vigilant swept forward and over the mega-city, passing over it in short minutes, its huge bulk displacing enough air to shake buildings and shatter glass. And that was before the steams of plasma blasted the air and anything else in their way out of existence.

"The way ahead is clear," declared the SAO.

"It's almost like they weren't expecting someone to do something completely insane," said Morix sarcastically.

"Commencing space-lane interface countdown. We'll be out of here in three minutes."

"Maintain PD-fire to our rear. Those support craft could still do some damage to the ship," warned Alanar.

The ship continued on over the landscape and eventually out into and through the atmosphere, opening an EP to the target location and heading through, leaving Second Hygra behind.

The *Vigilant Watchman* emerged moments later at the rendezvous points where all the other surviving craft had reassembled.

"Getting read-outs on the fleet," began Roaragh. "All ships...all ships are accounted for!"

"What!? Even the *Kanassit* and the *Plains*?" asked Alanar.

"Every ship reports heavy damage, but they are all here," confirmed the Kin-Sai.

It was a miracle. They had made it.

"Get me fleet-wide," ordered the Commodore.

"You have fleet-wide," said Morix a few seconds later.

"Attention all ships. This is Commodore Alanar," he began. "We have escaped the system with our objectives. Mission accomplished. Now let's regroup in convoy three formation and head home. The Confederation needs us now more than ever."

There were cheers and applause all over the ship and fleet from those who had survived.

"And to all Tardig boarders," he added, "I encourage you to surrender now. Your people may have forgotten how to fight honourably, but we have not."

He signalled for the termination of the link and turned to Morix.

"Get me status updates from all ships. I want to know what we have left, what we lost, who we saved – the works. I also need an uplink to the nearest Confederation formation. We need to find out what is going on."

The UIPE nodded and began processing the orders as the fleet assumed its formation. All they had to do was reach a Confederation outpost. Simple on paper but no-one knew how deep the enemy had gone into friendly space. They could have completely wiped out all resistance on the frontier by now. They would know soon enough.

"I'll be in the captain's office if anyone needs me," he told Roaragh before heading out of the C3C into the corridor. It seemed as though the entire ship was in ruins. Support columns had collapsed, deck plating buckled, screens had been smashed. He didn't really want to think about what Lal-ne-vo's office would look like.

He opened the door – or rather pried it open. Inside, ornaments had been overturned and knocked to the floor. The desk was still in place but the chairs lay strewn about the floor. Several plants were uprooted and soil scattered everywhere. It was a disaster area. Alanar picked up a chair and placed it back behind the desk before sitting in it, sighing heavily. It had been a long day.

The future now drew his attention. What would happen now to him, to the fleet, the Hygrans and the rest of the Confederation? All would probably be revealed on debriefing, including whether or not he would be condemned.

The door chimed.

"Enter," the Commodore said loudly, not bothering to turn and face the new arrival. He was far too tired.

"I'm assuming you haven't had time to redecorate yet?" asked a familiar female voice.

He looked to see Colony-Governor Akshell standing there in badly-tattered clothes, a pistol strapped to her side.

"How in the –" Alanar began, quickly getting to his feet.

"We had to evacuate the bunker when the landings began nearby," she explained, walking over and sorting a chair for herself. "Things looked bleak until we hooked up with the local Winn Winn force and they gave me a gun."

She motioned casually at the pistol.

"I tried to direct the colony from Paradise Plaza, but there was too much confusion for us to be effective. The Tardigs got most of my staff."

"They took out much of ours, too," Alanar commiserated. "They planned down to the last detail."

"How could this have happened?" the Colony-Governor demanded.

"We became too complacent and trusting. The Tardigs took advantage of that, striking us before we could react. They thought that taking out our frontier and part of the interior would cripple us and make us think twice about intervening to save the Winn Winn."

"Save them from what?"

"It appears the Republic annihilated the Winn Winn from many of their worlds and set them close to extinction," explained the Commodore "They feared we would not allow another genocide on our doorstep. Not after the Civil War."

Akshell nodded slowly.

"So they hit us first. My people. The colony. What do you think will happen now?"

"I imagine once they have secured all their objectives they'll sue for peace," Alanar suggested. "With our defences in ashes and whole worlds hostage, the Confederation will probably have to negotiate a settlement. My concerns are more immediate, however."

"Indeed, we need to get out of here." Akshell agreed before peering at the ground and at a glint of glass and liquid. She bent down and picked up a bottle, holding it to the light to read the label before laughing weakly.

"Well, I'll be damned!" she exclaimed and handed the bottle to Alanar. "I thought Talans didn't drink alcohol."

"What is vo – vodka?" asked the Alanar, curiously, taking the bottle.

"It's a Human beverage. One of the strongest."

He unscrewed the cap, sniffed and raised his eyebrows.

"Any glasses?"

"I'm not sure."

Morix's miniature self flared onto the desk.

"Commodore, we have a problem. Fifty Republic craft just entered the area and are on an intercept course!"

"Call combat stations and prepare to bug out," he ordered.

Both Hygrans stood and ran towards the C3C where a state of panic had descended.

"The SLIDEs still haven't recovered from their transit and only a few weapons are still functioning."

"Enemy will be in range in five minutes."

"Arm all available weapons! Throw the furniture at them if you have to!"

This couldn't be how it would end. They were so close to making it.

"Detecting thirty more EPs in our vicinity."

"Oh, come on. More of them?!" cried Akshell.

"No!" Morix declared triumphantly. "More of us."

Twenty shieldships and ten swordships came into view at that moment and began tearing into the Tardigs.
More whoops and cheers broke out across the fleet as the enemy was obliterated by the superior fire power and surprise of the Confederation force.

"Incoming transmission from the lead swordship."

"Put it on holo."

Seconds later a figure in full naval regalia was before them.

"This is Admiral Kisugi aboard the Confederation Navy swordship *Justice Hammer* to the Second Hygra taskforce. Good to see you made it out. Your orders are to accompany this extraction force out of the area to the Uberon system for debriefing."

"Yes, Sir," saluted Alanar. "May I request a situation report?"

"It's a mess everywhere between here and Axiom, Commodore. They got us good," declared Kisugi.

"Succinct enough for you?"

"Yes, Sir."

"Excellent! Now, get those engines up and running, and set a standard course for Uberon. We jump in ten minutes."

The link terminated and they continued to watch as Kisugi's ships decimated the enemy force.

"So, that's it," breathed Akshell. "It's over."

"Maybe the battle," said Morix, "but I have a feeling this is only just the beginning of the war."

*   *   *

It took a full day to reach the Uberon system, the fleet jumping from what seemed to be one war zone to the next. Radio silence had been imposed and the only information came from rumours whispered between crews.

Some said the Republic had achieved total victory nearly everywhere with dozens of star systems falling under their control. Others said the Navy had fallen back wholesale or had been completely wiped out.

When they arrived in the system the sight was uninspiring. It was part chaotic staging area, part repair yard, part refugee centre and part ship graveyard. Before they even had time to collect themselves, Kisugi issued more orders.
The Hygran vessels were to return to Hygra, the Confederation craft were to stay and all 'civilians' were to be offloaded.

Finally, Morix and Alanar were ordered to board a military transport to an unspecified location under armed guard. Shortly before they left, Alanar heard the High Controller had died. Hopefully, intelligence staff had secured the rest of the data. It was out of his hands now.

Once aboard the transport the pair were kept isolated from the crew and external contacts. The guards told them it was for security purposes but that only made the Hygran and UIPE more concerned.

Morix offered to hack the ships' systems, but Alanar didn't want to irritate the guards any more than they already appeared to be.

Several hours after departing and on the cusp of granting the UIPE permission to hack the network, one of the guards approached the pair in their quarters.

"We have arrived," the armoured Kin-Sai grunted gruffly. "Follow me."

"Where are we?" asked Alanar.

"Dock X-3521, Star Haven."

That was unexpected. Star Haven was literally and metaphorically the heart of the Confederation Navy. Its location was a closely-guarded secret from all but the most high-ranking staff. Here the Navy's starships were built and maintained in vast numbers, its weapons and support craft were developed and many of its officers were trained. It was magnificent.

They followed the guard off the transport to a mag-lev car that ran on rails down to another section of the docks. As Alanar looked out of the windows, he could see this was just a small part of one of the two gigantic complexes that ran around a Hygran-like planet. One orbited the equator, the other over the poles. Beyond this was a ring of heavily industrialised asteroids providing resources for the shipyards and in the distance hung one of the moons that Alanar knew orbited the planet.

Why were they here? What could the top brass have wanted to see them about in person?

The mag-lev came to a halt near a gunship landing pad. That was when Alanar realised it was deadly quiet. There was only one gunship on the pad and no starships in any of the berths nearby. They must have all been deployed on alert. Star Haven couldn't possibly be in danger, too?

They continued on to the gunship which lifted off and tore down to the surface, bursting through the clouds minutes later. It was raining heavily over the primary Navy command complex, fitting weather for a situation like this.

Once landed they were led into the massive domed building that was the Admiralty and to an office on the top level. The guard ushered them inside. Morix had been connected to Star Haven's hologrid the whole time. It was so advanced she could be projected like this inside any construction.

Inside, sat behind a huge ornate wooden desk, was a young man in a full Confederation Navy uniform wearing the braids of a High Admiral. Yet this Human could not be more than twenty-five years old. What was this?

"Ah, Commodore Alanar and Officer Morix29," the man said in an unexpectedly polished accent. "Please sit down. I apologise for the run around you've been given but security is vital."

Alanar took a seat before the High Admiral and Morix materialised next to him in sitting position.

"Forgive me, High Admiral, but you're not—"

"What you expected? No, I suppose not. For security reasons I have to use a set of avatars who volunteered for this position. But I still wanted to see you in person, so to speak."

Alanar raised an eyebrow but said nothing. Waiting.

"What happened out there, Commodore?" the avatar pressed.

And so Alanar told his story about the mission. How they had travelled to Second Hygra, rescued the survivors and gained access to the information on the Winn Winn exterminations. Then how the Republic had infiltrated the area and drawn out the supports and butchered them before seizing the system. He ended with the tale of the counter-attack and retreat.

The High Admiral was quiet for a long time, processing the information. A sad look formed quickly on the avatar's visage.

"If only we'd known sooner," he said, "we could have negotiated. Now, though, we are beyond that."

"What is happening out there, Sir?" asked Morix.

"Of course. I'm sorry I kept this from you for so long, but I worried it might colour your report. You understand we needed clarity?"

The pair nodded, waiting for the dreadful news to come.

"Second Hygra wasn't the only system to resist the invasion," the avatar continued. "A Confederation run agri-colony was a neighbouring world of Second Hygra."

"Golden Horizon," said Alanar, nodding.

"Indeed. We aren't clear on how they did it, but the Confederation security detachment – that is: *three* warships – along with a Colonial Diet security force and some trade ships managed to destroy much of the initial one hundred ship-strong occupation force."

"Rather than deploy a larger force, several hours later the Republic sent a megaship, Golden Horizon..."

The avatar looked away briefly.

"Apologies, this avatar had family there, I'm given to understand," explained the High Admiral, choking back tears.

"Golden Horizon was incinerated in a plasma fire-storm. No survivors have been reported."

Alanar's mouth fell open. An entire planet. Unique. Irreplaceable. Gone. The thought was almost unimaginable.

"Our last stalkerships confirmed it and the news was leaked by a swathe of traders and refugees from nearby worlds. The whole Confederation knows what happened."

"Five hours ago, through unanimous verdicts of the Presidium, Councillory, Diet and Parliament, war was declared on the Tardig Republic with unconditional surrender as the sole demand. We have superior firepower and forces, sufficient to take this all the way to Tardig Prime."

"What are our orders now, Sir?" asked Alanar.

"I'm promoting you to Captain for your service in Second Hygra with Morix as your second-in-command," decided the High Admiral. "You'll take command of the *Vigilant Watchman*. Get it fixed up and Admiral Kisugi will find you something to do. Keep yourself in one piece, Captain. We're going to need capable commanders like you and Morix in the days to come."

The two stood and saluted. The High Admiral avatar returned the gesture.

"The transport will take you to the *Watchman*. Dismissed – and good luck!"

Morix flared away, but Alanar stayed behind, mindful of a comment he had heard earlier.

"Sir?"

"Yes, Captain?"

"Before he died, the High Controller said to tell you something: that you were a worthy opponent. Does this mean anything?"

The avatar paused for a moment, as if caught off-guard, then smirked wryly.

"I think you've been privy to enough secret information of late, Captain," the High Admiral replied, saying nothing more.

Alanar left, finally connecting his synth-sym to the local data-net. War was everywhere in Confederation space. Tardig ships on joint operations with the Navy had engaged them in battle. Those moored on worlds like Earth and Centre Prime had launched strikes on local cities and forces. In the warzone of the frontier, millions – perhaps billions – were dying and the centrepiece was the charred husk of Golden Horizon.

Morix flared into existence on his shoulder.

"So, what now?" she asked in an almost bored manner.

"Now?" asked the new Captain rhetorically. "We take this fight to the enemy. We have a war to win."

"How heroic," the UIPE remarked wryly and they, like the rest of their civilisation, marched off to the drums of war.

END OF BOOK ONE

Printed in Great Britain
by Amazon